PUBLIC
LONELINESS
YURI GAGARIN'S CIRCUMLUNAR FLIGHT
GERALD
BRENNAN

Other titles in the series:

PUBLIC LONELINESS

YURI GAGARIN'S CIRCUMLUNAR FLIGHT

PART OF THE ALTERED SPACE SERIES

GERALD BRENNAN

TORTOISE BOOKS
CHICAGO, IL

I wake up.

I am lying on my back in the moon ship.

I am alone in the 7K-L1, stacked atop a Proton rocket at the firing range at Tyura-Tam.

It is finally the day.

I boarded the ship two hours ago. I had to crawl on a board, an actual wooden board, from the gantry through the access point in the launch shroud. (This mission has been planned in such haste that there's been little time to develop all the small extras, like a proper metal access ramp.) Then I had to drop through the moon ship's top hatch legs first, holding on to an actual rope rope while the technicians watched warily. Once I got settled and strapped in, we ran through communications checks with the ultra-high frequency antennas, but while monitoring the other systems someone saw a low pressure reading in the liquid oxygen tank on the Block-D stage. They told me to wait while they topped off the tank and monitored the pressure to make sure it wasn't a leak. And while they were doing that I had nothing to do and so I fell asleep. I was alone in the ship without even a porthole—they're covered until the shroud is jettisoned after launch—and I fell asleep.

A radio voice in my headset. Academician Mishin: "Cedar, this is Dawn-1." (The same call signs I had on East-1. The ground stations are always Dawn-1, Dawn-2, etc. And every cosmonaut has a code name. The others chose obvious ones—Falcon, Hawk, Eagle, Golden Eagle. But I am Cedar.)

"Dawn-1, this is Cedar. I am feeling good." It is at least more comfortable this time; I'm in cloth coveralls, rather than the pressure suit. "I am...well-rested. What is our status?"

"Cedar, it seems to be a faulty sensor. You are on fifteen-minute readiness."

"Very good, Dawn-1."

The mission has been prepared in utmost secrecy.

Yes, I went through the normal rituals—the trip to Red Square, to Lenin's Tomb and the Kremlin Wall—but in the predawn hours, so as not to be seen. Then back here to spend the night in the little white cottage with the metal frame bed and the bare wooden floor. The same place I slept six years and six months ago. The last night before everyone in the world knew my name. The last normal night of my life.

This time it was decided that there would be no whispers or rumors. No helpful hints to journalists that they should be prepared for a major announcement. There was an unmanned circumlunar test of the 7K-L1/Proton combo six weeks ago, but as far as the outside world is concerned, this is just another test. A ship with a mannequin stuffed with radiation sensors broadcasting taped messages. Another Ivan Ivanovich. The decision was made in a late-night meeting of the State Commission after prodding from on high; it was followed up with decrees stamped: DO NOT DISPLAY. DISSEMINATION PER LIST. And the lists have been short.

The announcement will come via television when I am coming around the moon. And of course then it will be too late for anyone to do anything about it. They will broadcast my face from the capsule and live pictures of the moon from my ship and everyone will know that I was first, that a Soviet man was first. And Yuri Levitan will read it out on the radio. And the people will cheer, again.

(Surely that's the best way to do it. Why announce it ahead of time? At best, everything goes as planned, and where's the excitement in that? Or perhaps there is a little bit of drama, some unexpected deviation from the plan. And while that gets people interested, it also makes the planners look foolish. But to announce that it is done, that the planners worked in secrecy and executed everything perfectly and now, right now, there is a real man, a Soviet citizen, rounding the moon...surely that's the best way to do it.)

"Cedar, give us a reading on your environmental systems." Mishin says. He is on the radio supervising everything, just as Korolev was on that famous morning. With Korolev—Sergei Pavlovich—I had a natural affinity. I was the son he wanted. He was the father I could look up to. Mishin and I have no such relationship. I am the wayward son; he's the father who worries he isn't getting enough respect. But it is sometimes convenient to copy the shape of past things, even when the feeling is wrong.

I scan the gauges. "Cabin pressure—one atmosphere. Humidity—60. Temperature—20 degrees."

"Very good. Ten-minute readiness."

There were plans to launch the Union instead, in April—to send it on its maiden voyage with Komarov at the helm. Then we would have launched another, so they could rendezvous in space in advance of the May Day celebrations. Certainly we've gotten used to being first—the first satellite, the first man in space, the first woman, the first man to walk in space, and so on. And this would have been the first physical docking of two manned spacecraft. A union of Unions! What's more, we would have had a transfer between the two ships, to send two men back in a different craft than they'd launched in.

But White Tass has been full of black news. The American Gemini program has been a tremendous success. And despite recent setbacks, they're still on track to go to the moon with Apollo. Such brashness—to say such things in public, then follow through! It's like playing against a basketball team that diagrams their plays on a chalkboard for all to see, but is so powerful that one ends up falling behind regardless. The only tactic against such an adversary is cunning and guile. You can't try to imitate them—that's the surest path to defeat. Plus, there were glitches with the Union that could not be resolved in time. So Komarov's mission was cancelled.

It was by no means certain we'd be able to do something better. Sergei Pavlovich's death last year was a great blow. But Mishin is a competent engineer. Whatever his failings as a leader, we are here, and it is time to do this. Plus, we're not using Korolev's boosters this time around. Before Khrushchev's fall, Chelomey had secured the necessary decrees to develop the Proton rocket strapped to my back, and to initiate development work on a circumlunar flight.

So we have been laying the groundwork for this for some time. And when news came of the Apollo fire—well, certainly it was sad, and humbling. There is a level I hope beyond politics or ideology where we all can mourn such things. For us at Star City—once Kilometer 41, once the Green City—it was particularly sobering. This was, after all, the first loss of life in a spacecraft—a clear reminder that death haunts this business, that someday we will lose someone during an actual spaceflight. But after the initial pang of emotion, there always comes the calculated thought. And that was: we have some breathing room. They've stumbled, and we can pull back ahead.

And so, the decision: to launch the circumlunar flight in October 1967, to coincide with both the 10th anniversary of our first satellite and the 50th anniversary of the October Revolution. A triumph that will call to mind past triumphs, while also surpassing them.

"Five-minute readiness, Cedar."

"Understood. I am feeling well."

Switches and gauges. Knobs and buttons. The little globe under glass. Everything looks fine. Underneath I feel uncertainty. We have prepared in haste. But everything looks the way it is supposed to.

"One minute readiness, Cedar."

This is what I want to hear. I smile, though I don't know if the camera can see it. "I am ready."

I have been waiting for this day for two thirds of a decade. Waiting for this moment. There is no countdown for our launches. The final seconds are falling away without a sound.

Then, from Mishin: "Feed one." Starting telemetry. Graph paper rolling underneath pens drawing peaks and valleys. "Key in launch position. Vent." The launch commands are enabled. The moon ship is ready. "Feed two." Backup telemetry.

And at last: "Launch."

Beneath me pumps are opening. The rocket is waking up. Nitrogen tetroxide and heptyl igniting on contact. Toxic dragon chemicals. Brownish-yellow clouds I cannot see. And fire.

A rumble rises through my back, and the hairs on my arm go to gooseflesh, and the rocket starts its shuddering rise, and over the noise I hear the radio voice: "Liftoff." And I'm being pressed down into the launch couch, but I find myself shouting: "Here we go again!"

The rocket pushes relentlessly. Soon my chest is tight. But I am mindful of the controllers and I want to reassure them. "I am fine, I am in excellent spirits, the rocket is working perfectly." I feel like I'm repeating myself from last time. But it is just as well. Radio dialogue is boring. We speak in short sentences and convey only the necessary information. Maybe a few banalities. We can talk at length later. At any rate I'm too excited to be profound.

There is a jolt as the second stage ignites. Then the pyrotechnic bolts fire and the first stage falls away. My eyes scan the mission clock. Just over two minutes have elapsed. I've been worried about Chelomey's rocket, but it is doing everything it's supposed to do. And Glushko's engines are working perfectly. "Staging complete," I call out.

It may disappoint you to learn that nobody really flies a rocket into orbit. The gyroscopes and fuel pumps and ignition timers are calibrated to do nearly everything, so we are reduced to monitoring the systems. My fragile life is perched precariously atop a flaming pedestal which at any moment could topple, crushing and incinerating me, sending my shattered blackened bones falling to the Kazakh steppe. I may have a second or two to avoid that fate by pulling the handle on the escape tower, which will pull my spacecraft free from the presumably exploding booster. So I must keep my eyes on the gauges. Other than reporting on my status, this is my only task: to be prepared. To be, in general, rather than to do.

My body shakes as the rocket rumbles beneath me. But soon there is a pleasant smoothness. Steady acceleration. Less buffeting. The atmosphere is getting thinner. I am riding into space on a pillar of fire.

(My life has been forged by fire—a childhood in the Great Patriotic War, a youth at the foundry at Lyubertsy, an adulthood perched at the end of various jet engines. Then with East-1, you might say I was born again of fire. And now this.)

Now comes a whoosh as the escape tower pulls away. The launch shroud falls off and I can see my first glimpses outside: the arc of clouds and the darkening sky.

•••

Before I continue, I should at least ask: who are you?

In the isolation chamber, before East-1, I prided myself on knowing who I was talking to. They sent me in for two weeks. Two weeks locked behind a giant steel door in front of a one-way mirror, with them keeping an eye on my every move, and me just sitting there in a chair. (Oh, there were tasks— panels and buttons. And meals—squeezable tubes of meat and cheese paste. But it was tremendously boring. Again, just sitting there *being*.)

Kamanin, the director of our flight training, had orchestrated these intense periods of observation. He was (and of course still is) a general, an accomplished aviator, the very first Hero of the Soviet Union—and an unrepentant Stalinist, with the consequent obsession to keep an eye on people. Public loneliness, the watchers called it. They wanted to watch you without you watching them.

So I was stuck in there, observed and isolated, with little to do but go on about my duties. And I found myself singing— composing odes to my tubes of food, little ditties to keep my spirits up. Yes, singing to my food!

> *Tubes of glorious socialist cheese!*
> *You empty yourselves to fill us up!*
> *You must have read what Marx once said:*
> *To each according to his need!*
>
> *New Soviet cheese!*
> *So nourishing to me!*
> *You must be heeding Kamanin's words:*
> *To Yuri according to his need!*

I pretended to be lost in my isolation, but I heard a chuckle— a stifled little transmitted laugh—before they cut the microphone. And it seemed like something that would put me in good standing—just the right mix of political ardor and political humor.

More importantly, I knew I could get away with it, for I knew who was in the control room! I had memorized the names of all the watchers! I had procured a work schedule—never you mind how!—and studied it, hard-wired it into the circuitry of my brain along with all the rocket specifications and capsule diagrams we also had to learn. And I was able to call them out at every shift change, with name and patronymic. Greetings, Ivan Pavlovich! Greetings, Pavel Ivanovich! And—well, how could they not be impressed? This always gets people's attention—when they think they have arranged a certain number of outcomes, and they try to compel you to pick from among those outcomes, and you instead engineer something else through naked determination.

Which is what I've done again, with this moon mission. I've clawed my way out of the spotlight and back into the cockpit. I'm a different man: not the perfect Soviet specimen I once was. Thinner hair, thicker waist. A scar on my eyebrow—never mind how it got there. What matters is where I am now. Despite the petty jealousies of nameless adversaries, I've made it back to where I wanted to be all along.

I trust you're happy for me. Do you feel a certain kinship with me, a certain bond? Perhaps you've been studying facts of my life, everything you don't know about Yuri Gagarin: where I was born, where I went to school, and so forth. You might be looking for similarities between yourself and me—a shared birthday, or even just a Zodiac sign, if you believe in that sort of thing. Maybe you're trying to analyze my name—Yuri, derived from George, like Georgy and Yegor—to see if my birthday is your name-day, or vice versa. You could even be looking at political and religious issues: searching for proof that I'm a committed atheist, or a closet Christian; a good Russian son of the soil, or a secret admirer of the West; a sincere Soviet, or one who quietly questions the regime. Or perhaps you're just looking at certain traits of mine and telling yourself they're yours as well: intelligence, courage, determination, humor under pressure.

If so, I can certainly understand it—I'm not trying to criticize you! To be human—there is always that longing for connection. And especially with someone like me, someone who's done some remarkable thing, there is that hope for something shared. (Unless you're sure we have nothing in common, in which case you're perhaps looking to downplay my accomplishments, to find proof that I'm not worthy of the praises I've been given.) I hope I'm not putting words in your mouth! I'm not trying to be rude; I just want to speculate for a bit. You're perhaps looking for these connections, trying to see a bit of you in me, so you can see a bit of me in you. It's quite all right! I've done the same thing with my heroes: Heroes of the Soviet Union like Alexey Maresyev, Nikolai Gastello and Alexander Matrosov; pioneers of rocketry like Korolev and Tsiolkovsky; even literary heroes, particularly the various characters from Tolstoy.

I am eager to tell some stories—not just about this flight, but also about my life. (Yes, I've already written my autobiography, but there are always certain strictures to be observed in such a setting. And I was hoping for another flight, so I had no interest in saying absolutely everything. Is that dishonest? I don't think so. It's normal to present the best side of yourself when you're trying to gain favor. You surely do the same thing when you're getting to know someone but you don't quite know if you can trust them— on a date, perhaps, or while trying to secure employment.)

Still, you have me at a disadvantage. You know who I am— everyone does. I'm a real man. A Soviet man, a Russian. But I have no idea whether you are communist or capitalist, atheist or Christian or Moslem or Jew. How can I know what stories to tell if I don't know who you are?

But perhaps it doesn't matter. If you're even remotely curious about what it means to be a real man, surely this story will interest you.

●●●

When the Block-D stage finishes I feel a familiar shift in my body against the straps. Again I am weightless. There is no time to get unstrapped—we have less than one orbit to prepare before the Block-D will reignite for the next firing, the big one, the one that will send me moonward. But after that, I will have time to enjoy the feeling at last.

The solar panels deploy automatically, which then clears the way for the stellar alignment system to work. Everything unfolding in sequence like a mechanical flower.

"Dawn-2, this is Cedar. Dawn-2, this is Cedar." Now that we've launched, I'm no longer talking to Tyura-Tam but instead communicating via relay with the new control center in the Crimea.

"Go ahead, Cedar." Blondie's voice! Just like before! I was delighted and now I'm overjoyed.

"Dawn-2...Blondie...We have first cosmic velocity." The spacecraft's most important instruments are simple gauges, not unlike a car speedometer. Except if the needles are moving, something's wrong. But everything's steady. "All temperature and pressure readings are normal. Both panels are deployed. We are drawing electricity at 27 volts, 25 amps."

"Very good. Verify functioning of the ionic and attitude systems."

"Ionic system is working properly. I am oriented 20 degrees relative to the orbital path." I give a quick pulse of the peroxide thrusters. Short movements with the right-hand controller—back and forth in each axis. This is the first time I've actually controlled a spacecraft. It is sluggish with the Block-D stage attached. But working as expected. "DO system is responsive."

"Very good, Yura." (Yura's my nickname. No shorter, so you can't really call it a diminutive. But I guess at 157 centimeters I'm small enough already.) "The ballistics center is verifying your orbit."

"Very well. I am turning control of the craft over to the 100-K system so it can initiate a roll about the solar axis." On East-1, the spacecraft oriented itself using optical sensors that found the horizon on every side. Here we also have star sensors and can direct the ship to point itself at the sun and the moon, so we know it knows where it is. But in this mode, the solar axis rotation, the system puts the spacecraft in a constant roll.

From Blondie: "Tracking your orbital parameters as follows. Perigee 191.3 kilometers. Apogee 221 kilometers. Inclination is 51 degrees, 44 minutes. Period is 88 minutes. All within normal limits. How's the view, Yura?"

"Not as good as you had, I'm sure!" (Blondie was the first man to leave his ship and float freely in space, back on Sunrise-2. In case you don't know, it was a dangerous mission. A truly heroic flight, far more demanding than mine was.)

"You'll get to go outside up there someday, Yura."

"I'll settle for the moon, Blondie."

He laughs. We both know he may get to go outside there, too. It's looking like he'll be leading the contingent of cosmonauts training for lunar landings. Assuming the N-1/L-3 combo comes together, he will captain the first mission. And I do hope it happens. I'd love to land myself, but seeing such a good friend accomplish such a feat is surely the next best thing.

Still, we've said enough over the open channel. My orbit has me skimming over the top of Mongolia and cutting through Manchuria, then back over our land. But that will be brief; the globe indicator shows I'll soon be crossing the coast near Vladivostok. And we all know the C.I.A. has ships prowling the waters of the East Sea. They'll know I'm up here, and depending on their monitoring on the other side of the globe, they may soon know where I'm going. Will they make it public before we do? Trumpet our triumph, and their shame? That's the great uncontrollable factor in all this. We'll find out soon enough.

There is a lot to be done before this orbit is complete. We must make sure the buffer batteries are providing a constant electrical current, even when the ship and the solar panels are rotating, or when we're in Earth's shadow. And after this morning's issues, we must carefully monitor the pressure in the Block-D stage. We don't want to head for the moon if there are problems. Still I can't help stealing glimpses of the wondrous view out my portholes. The sky looks overcast (or undercast for me, I suppose), so I can't tell exactly where I cross the coast. But the weather starts to break apart, and soon I can see the beautiful blue sea far below.

(Back in 1961, Sergei Pavlovich penned an article under an assumed name for the newspaper *Truth* that said: "Soviet soil is now the shoreline of the universe." A grandiose statement, perhaps; a triumph of socialist realist rhetoric. I don't know that he'd have praised the system that fervently in private—as the old joke goes, there is no truth in *Truth*. Still, I think of it now, and how it's coming true, and how I wish he were here to see it.)

Now below I can see the shadowed outlines of the lingering clouds. Then Honshu, turning autumn brown. And before long I am heading into darkness. I'm tempted to reorient myself, but I don't want to waste fuel on unnecessary maneuvers. Still I do crane my neck to see something I've been missing these last few years, even though I only saw it once: the orbital sunset.

And now, heading southeast across the Pacific, it is upon me. There is darkness above and below: two oceans, one infinitely vast. And a few brilliant arcs of light, split by an atmospheric prism into reds and salmons and oranges. I watch until the sun winks out.

•••

It's perhaps natural to think back to my first flight. Surely you want to know about that.

Again, I spent that fateful April night in Sergei Pavlovich's cottage. The bare room with the metal frame bed. Nothing special. After my flight it was invested with meaning. It became the room where everyone had to spend the night before their flight. In the absence of God, the state makes its own rituals.

In the morning I woke and ate breakfast from tubes: meat and marmalade. Getting my stomach used to what I'd be eating up there. Then they drove me to the center. I remember Sergei Pavlovich's wide face, exhausted but beaming. His dark intelligent eyes, so often sad, were now joyful. (He chose me first, before Khrushchev. And by then we knew that our fates and our names would be forever linked, even though his wouldn't be public for a while.) I put on the blue pressure garment, and then the orange coverall that everyone remembers, and the white helmet with the red letters, freshly painted: C.C.C.P. I remember grinning at my reflection. Everything looked sharp.

I headed out to a blue and white bus, customized with two wide seats. All around were technicians. But not all were there for a purpose. Some were just trying to see. And of course there were photographers. A small taste of things to come.

Titov was on the bus already, sitting towards the back. Suited up like me. We'd only known for a few days that I would be flying and he would be backing me up. When I boarded, we exchanged pleasantries. Banalities. We were not positioned to be able to talk to one another after that. Was he hoping something would go wrong with my suit? A rip, a tear, nothing serious, but big enough to make them replace me with him? I can forgive him for those dark unspoken thoughts. Everyone wants to be first in our line of work.

Then the long silent ride to the launch pad. Staring out at the railcars full of kerosene and the endless grassy plain. On a morning such as that, even the empty steppe looks beautiful and golden.

I knew that, if everything went well, I would not have a lot to do. The spacecraft was designed to stay under automatic guidance for the duration of the flight. The Americans had recruited experienced test pilots for their astronaut corps, but we were plucked from the ranks of the air force. So every cosmonaut in those early days was a junior fighter pilot. And it occurred to someone that if we had manual controls we could do something wrong and bring the spacecraft down somewhere other than the planned spot, and possibly even miss the Soviet Union entirely. Make a mess of all the well-laid plans. Turn the state's great triumph into a worldwide embarrassment.

(This is how the thinking goes. The apparatus of fear: concerned not so much with doing things as with preventing things. It's ugly and limited, like the scaffolding of the launch tower next to the rocket. These days I sometimes wonder if it will fall away in time. But it has been a necessary part of the journey.)

Of course, the engineers knew we needed a manual option. They figured there would be a failure somewhere, and if it happened in the automatic system and I couldn't fire the retrorockets, I'd be stuck up there in orbit until my food and water and oxygen ran out. Like Laika. An animal with no way to come home.

So: a compromise. They designed the manual controls to be unlocked with a combination, which they would then read to me over the radio if something went wrong. Assuming the radio was working correctly.

It was not my biggest concern, but it was there. A thought out of place like a pebble in my shoe.

But as I waddled from the bus to the rocket, Sergei Pavlovich came up for some last words. He leaned in close so no one could hear. I expected fatherly advice, but he said: "Yura, we put an envelope with the code to the manual controls inside the craft. And…well, if you can't reach it, the combination is 1-2-5. Got it?"

"Got it. 1-2-5." I smiled.

"All right, my little falcon." He patted my shoulder and lingered for a second. A lifetime of hopes and dreams in his tired eyes. Then he receded through the crowd, headed for the bunker.

There was movement in the mass of people. Ivanovsky, anxious. (In case you don't know, he was lead engineer for the ship, working under Feoktistov.) There was something he needed to say, a hot coal in his mouth he needed to spit out. He pulled me towards the ladder and cupped his hand over his mouth. Then he, too, whispered in my ear the three numbers.

"Got it," I said with a nod.

"That's it?" He seemed to think I was insufficiently grateful—which was understandable. He was risking his career to give me information that might save my life.

"Korolev told me already." I grinned. (You can't discuss the foibles of the lowly with the mighty. But to do the opposite is all right.)

He, too, smiled and gave me a pat on the shoulder.

Then came the ladder to the elevator. Green steel. As solid as my confidence. I clambered up excitedly, with Ivanovsky backwards in front of me, waiting to offer a helping hand. The support arms clasped the rocket above us, creating the illusion of a soaring interior space. Awe-inspiring, like a metal cathedral.

Up top, I turned to wave to everyone before I got into the elevator. I was surprised: so many smiles! Surely they all knew I would not be up there without all of them. But they seemed genuinely happy. Glad to be part of something so great. They knew my life was in their hands, so my hopes were their hopes.

Then the elevator door closed and I left them behind. Watched through the round window as they got smaller and the ground fell away. The start of my ascent.

And then the capsule. Its gleaming circular hatch. The portal to my future. When I went in everything was the same as it had always been. But I knew when I came back through it everything would be strange and new.

I put my hand on the rim of the hatch as I climbed in. Saw my gloved fingers against the capsule's green skin. I remember thinking: this will be in space. Then burned by the atmosphere. Although I knew it, it did not seem possible. But nothing happens without change.

Once on my back in the capsule I settled in. Shifted my weight around. By then it was all comfortable and familiar. The pale green interior. The little control boxes with their switches and dials. The globe.

Ivanovsky was above me, his narrow diamond face upside-down in the circular hatch. He explained again the communications tests we needed to run. The blockhouse was Dawn-1, Kopashevo was Dawn-2, and Elizovo was Dawn-3. We'd run through it already, but it was a welcome refresher. And he kept talking, bringing up last-minute issues. On a project this big everyone has thoughts and tips and suggestions that have been lingering in the corners of their mind like lint.

At last he pulled back, replaced by: Kamanin.

The general leaned in close. "I don't know if I should tell you this, but the combination to the manual controls is 1-2-5."

"Got it," I said, smiling so hard it hurt. A real, genuine smile. Gagarin, the laughing one. This is who I was, who I still am. This is what they expected from me. What they still expect. "Thank you, sir."

Ivanovsky stepped back up and armed my ejection seat.

For a long time after they closed the hatch I was talking to Korolev in the blockhouse. Communicating and identifying issues. I gave them readings on temperature and humidity. They had to fix a problem with the hatch sensors. In the meantime they piped music in: songs about love. I was feeling good. Ready to start.

As this went on, they announced the readiness. One-hour readiness. Ten-minute readiness. One-minute readiness.

Then they said they were giving the signals to start the ignition and I heard valves opening beneath me and there was a rumbling and a growing noise. And in the middle of that I realized I was feeling the rocket rise.

"Here we go!" I called out. (Or so they told me—I don't remember it, but there it is on the tapes, my voice!) "Everything is going well, I am feeling fine, I'm in a cheerful mood, everything is normal."

From the ground: "We all wish you a good flight!" To which I replied: "Goodbye! See you soon, dear friends!"

And the rumble continued and there was an anxious voice in the headset as I rose: Korolev kept asking me how I was feeling—he was a nervous wreck!

And it occurred to me, there on the rocket, that he hadn't slept a wink. "I'm fine," I yelled over the noise. "How are you feeling?"

The g-forces were making it difficult to speak, and there was a bright light for the television camera in my face. But I made sure to keep telling them I was feeling fine.

Then came a quiver beneath me as the four booster blocks separated. Nothing unexpected. And the nosecone, the protective covering, separated as planned three minutes in to the flight, and I peered through the porthole and saw dark blue sky and thought: It is real, it is happening. I will be the first.

More g-forces. Old Number Seven was working exactly as it was supposed to, or so it seemed. And the central core fell off and there was another lurch and I rode the upper stage to orbit.

Soon the vibrations and the g-forces were gone. Everything had fallen away. There were still the familiar noises of pumps and fans, and the same side panel with its switches and the front panel with its dials and globe, but it all felt different. Although I was strapped in tightly, I felt my arms floating up and my torso moving against the straps.

Just like that, I had gone from being just another earthbound mortal, to something else entirely: the first. Only nine short minutes had passed. And I'd done nothing. They'd strapped me in and I'd read the gauges and told them I was feeling good—but I'd done nothing! Another Ivan Ivanovich, a mannequin with a pulse. Surely you can understand why I felt a little awkward after that, a little humble, certainly, compared to someone like Alexey Maresyev, a real hero who was shot down by the Germans and lost both legs and went through the trouble of getting cleared to fly again so as to get back to killing Germans. How could I compare with that? (If you don't like me and have nothing in common with me, perhaps you're latching on to this fact, the fact that I did nothing, as proof that I'm not as impressive as all the posters and parades would suggest!) Nine minutes. How often in your life has so much changed in so short a time?

•••

But I'm in a new spacecraft now. Manual controls. The chance to really fly. The only thing I've wanted all along. (I have that in common with Maresyev, at least!)

My path slashes across Chile and Argentina. In the orbital night I can see stars, stars, stars: clusters and clumps, and the bright swath of the galaxy. More stars than you have ever seen on the clearest darkest night on Earth. And I'm headed northeast across the Atlantic for the final burn. Second cosmic velocity.

"This is Cedar, this is Cedar."

Somewhere in the dark ocean, the relay ships are re-transmitting my signal to Yevpatoriya. I hear a slight delay, then Blondie's voice, crackly: "Cedar, this is Dawn-2."

"Dawn-2, I am just about to head back into daylight." I scan my panel. "Buffer batteries have been working as expected. Electrical current is still 25 amperes, 27 volts. Realigning with the 100-K."

Again, a transmission: crackly, inaudible. There are strange readings on the ionic control system. My globe indicator shows I'm off the South American coastline.

"Dawn-2, I am passing through the Brazilian Magnetic Anomaly. Please repeat your transmission."

I hear something that sounds like: We are monitoring your telemetry. Everything is as expected.

And now: orbital sunrise. I feast my eyes on it, for I may not see it on the way home.

I am moving faster than the planet spins. So my sunrise is Earth's sunset. The effect is the same as before, only in reverse: I see arcs of color appear in the blackness and then swell as the sun fills the center. And then I must look away, for the sun, once it is up above the horizon, is even brighter than on Earth, more brilliant than you can imagine, impossibly bright against the black sky. One of those incomparably strange things: to have full sunlight when the sky looks like night.

And then I'm across the terminator and the Atlantic is beneath me, bright blue. Very few clouds today.

"Yura, you have go-ahead for Block-D firing," I hear. "Ten minutes to go."

This is the big new thing. What nobody has done before. If something had gone wrong they could have held me back. But they haven't.

The big computers downstairs have been spinning. Vacuum tubes and lights and mechanical contraptions churning out calculations. Blondie reads out the expected values for the burn time and delta-v based on my orbit. The sun is rising higher in the black sky. There is still some static and I have him re-read the values before I'm content that I've heard them correctly.

The burn will take place over the Gulf of Guinea. That last little bight of the Atlantic Ocean. The armpit of Africa.

"Five minutes to go."

I key in commands to stop the solar rotation and align the spacecraft for the burn. The ionic control system is still acting strangely, but the 100-K tells me I'm properly oriented.

I transmit: "I'm ready up here."

I am excited, even though I know how final this will be. During East-1, if something had gone wrong I would have at least returned to Earth eventually. But on this mission, once I hit second cosmic velocity I will be leaving the planet behind. Trusting my life yet again to equations and calculations, scribblings on forgotten chalkboards and discarded pieces of graph paper. The spacecraft will have to stay on course and approach the moon at just the right angle and in just the right spot so that the lunar gravity will send me whipping around back to Earth. We will of course be able to make a couple of mid-course corrections. But at best, it will be six days until I can make it home, and if I'm not on a very narrow course, I will not be able to survive reentry. Still, I think of the years when it seemed like I would never make it back up here. And I am here and it is real and I am excited.

"One minute."

I see the seconds count down.

Then the rocket ignites. Gravity returns and I am pressed back into my form-fitting couch and I watch the timer climb. White numbers on black dials, like the odometer on a car, counting seconds towards the magic number: 459. Watching, watching, watching. Will something go wrong even now? At 440, I bring my hand up to the control panel. If the rocket keeps firing past the appointed time I will need to cut it off manually. Everything has been calculated precisely, but if it is executed sloppily it will all be for naught.

But right on schedule the numbers stop spinning. Again I feel my body rise against the straps.

"Second cosmic velocity," I transmit.

"We concur. Everything appears nominal. Cedar, you have go-ahead to jettison the Block-D stage."

"Jettisoning Block-D stage," I say. It doesn't seem enough. So I add: "We're on our way to the moon!" Even though I'm the only one up here.

●●●

Near the end of East-1, I knew I was in trouble.

That orbit had been at a higher inclination, about 65 degrees. It had taken me arcing up towards the Arctic, avoiding Japan, then down across the Pacific, missing South America by swooping below Cape Horn and over the Antarctic Peninsula. Then up across the South Atlantic for reentry. Geography being what it is—the area of knowledge that most thoroughly resists state decrees and revisions—the craft had to begin those procedures over Africa. (As a young man, I took all of this without question. But looking back, I can't escape the nagging thought: it was as if they wanted added redundancy for the combination lock on the manual controls. They didn't even trust me to fly over any place where I might be tempted to land!)

So I was passing over Africa when I started my trip back to Earth. And I was thinking of my mother, my dear mother. (When we'd last talked, I'd told her I was in training, but I hadn't told her what for. And I'd told her I'd be taking a trip, but when she'd asked what kind of trip, I'd simply said "A long one!" So I was wondering what she'd think—here I was at the tail end of the longest and fastest trip ever taken by a man!) And it seemed like it was all happening according to plan, precisely controlled by timers and clocks. I did not know that there already was one problem—Old Number Seven had burned for too long, so my orbit was higher than expected, so I was coming down off-target. The relay ships had neglected to pass that information along.

And soon there was a problem that launch control couldn't conceal. This may be your first time hearing about it—I did not discuss it in my memoir, for reasons which should soon be apparent—but I swear that this time I'm telling the full truth.

The retro-rocket pack fired normally, creating an artificial gravity that pushed me back into the couch. Then there was a sharp jolt as the four explosive devices fired to sever the metal straps holding the TDU—the instrument module—to the reentry module, the metal sphere in which I sat. And as it happened there was a violent twisting of the ship, and the lights on my instrumentation panel went off—but they came on again.

The instrument signals came via an umbilical cable that went from the TDU to the reentry module, so it was obvious at once what had happened: the cable was still attached. It was supposed to be severed via a guillotine device, and the instrument module was supposed to fall away so the heat shield could take the brunt of reentry.

The craft started to spin, faster and faster and faster. And I could tell it was not a simple spin: I was rotating about all three axes. And I could hear the retro-pack banging against the hull of my craft! I hoped the umbilical cord would give way soon, but it occurred to me that it might not happen soon enough. And the black of space outside the portholes had been replaced by a plasma glow, an orange-pink furnace just centimeters from my face, hotter than any foundry I'd seen.

I could feel the air getting warner in my ship. It was not my imagination! I had dropped the faceplate visor and was sealed up in my pressure suit and still I could feel myself getting warmer.

I told myself not to worry; I remembered the forge at Lyubertsy, and how the foreman had told us not to fear the incandescent sparks, the rivers of molten steel. "Fire is strong," he'd said. "But water is stronger than fire, and earth is stronger than water. And man is the strongest of all."

Finally the cable gave way, and I heard a last mighty *thud* against the side of my ship—but the capsule started spinning faster! And the gravitational forces pinned me against my couch and I felt pressure in my head and saw my vision fading.

But then the rotation slowed.

At last the capsule was reentering properly, and it had been weighted and balanced so as to fall in a stable manner. I monitored the gauges: pressure normal; temperature above normal, but coming down.

Now I was feeling good. I had my wits about me. I had come through the worst part, the great unknown. True, it hadn't gone as expected, but everything was designed well enough to handle a little abnormality. My portholes were streaked with burn marks, but the ship had held together. The sky was blue again. The capsule felt comfortable and familiar.

Boom! The hatch blew off.

Instantly everything was bright and smoky and there was a circle of sky where the hatch had been. This was as expected—we had been training for it—but still it was jarring in the moment. I felt naked, exposed.

I tensed myself.

My ejection seat fired, hurtling me out of my cozy capsule and into the empty sky.

•••

Ever since that last flight I've been waiting to be truly weightless, waiting to feel free. For space travel comes at a cost: you get a short wondrous time where everything feels infinite, then it's off into a gilded cage, a public prison of sorts, in which your own unique experiences keep you confined.

The important thing is that I've escaped that—escaped everything, really—and now at last I can be free. Like Maresyev, I've fought hard to climb back into the cockpit. I may not have had as many obstacles, nor have mine been as daunting, but that is how it goes. You do not choose your obstacles; they line up before you, seemingly of their own volition.

After the burn, they radio up telemetry. Delta-v values and expected times for the mid-course correction. Dutifully, I copy it all down.

And now at last I can unstrap myself. Leave my couch behind.

I'm grinning as I undo the buckles. My body rises of its own accord. I have floated in aircraft, brief parabolas in empty Tupolevs that reeked of poorly-cleaned vomit, but here there will be no sudden buffets throwing me towards the walls, no buzzers and lights reminding me to float back down to the floor in thirty seconds lest I come crashing down after the pilots start pulling up. Everything smells fresh and new—or perhaps I'm imagining. (Your sinuses get fuller in zero gravity. They don't drain, and there's a puffiness to your face.) Still, I'm thrilled. All those years of gymnastics—here at last I can tumble freely!

Or try to, anyway. The cabin feels somewhat larger now, but it is still not roomy, even solo. Two and a half cubic meters. I consider doing a somersault, but realize in short order I don't have space. Even reorienting's problematic; attempting to reverse myself, I bang my head against the panel and go ricocheting off. Still, it's fun and good—like being drunk in three dimensions! Some have complained about nausea, especially when floating free, but I'm fine.

I peer out of the porthole. The Block-D stage is falling behind but still visible, bright and sharp in the sunlight. Dawn-2 transmitted a command for it to fire its thrusters briefly, and I pulsed my controls to get a little extra separation, but given the realities of orbital mechanics, it'll be following me around the moon.

I cannot see my destination. Right now it's blocked by the bulk of the spacecraft. But beyond the Block-D stage I now have a full view of Earth, half-shadowed, gleaming, round and big like a basketball in front of your face when you're getting ready to pass—a massive ball of water and cloud and ice, slowly getting smaller.

• • •

When my ejection seat finally separated, I was suspended in the sky under a beautiful full parachute.

Any misgivings I'd had about the reentry had fallen away with my craft. I was in my element—the only phase of the flight we'd been able to practice, rather than simulate. And not only had we spent months parachuting, we'd been trained to recognize geography from the air, to know where we were by sight. But it turned out I had no need—this was familiar! I was coming down near Saratov—which was where I'd learned to fly not all that many years before. (Those years were as close in time to East-1 as East-1 is to me now.) This was not as expected—it was better than expected!

I'd ejected at an altitude of several kilometers, so I was a long time floating down. And as my body slowly fell, my spirits swiftly rose. Everything had fallen into place. Even the dangerous tumbling reentry now felt right, for it had heightened the drama, and given me cause to feel I'd really risked something, really accomplished something. And now, this—the familiar farmlands, the city by the river, the mighty Volga shimmering beyond. I hadn't been back since those flying club days, and it felt like a homecoming. Another circle completed.

I floated down into a field. Saw the soil rising until at last it was there. I landed so gently I didn't even need to fall and roll.

I remember thinking: it's done. It's done, and it can never be undone.

As I gathered my parachute about me, I saw a woman and child. I waved to them. They eyed me with suspicion—my face plate was down and we could not make eye contact. Then a farmer came up behind them—a very confused farmer! Yuri Levitan had announced my flight over the radio when I was just about to reenter—they'd broadcast it nationwide on our radios, those radios that couldn't be turned off, the ones that sent the same news into every apartment and office and factory—and the country was starting to rejoice. My mother and my wife were at last learning the truth about my trip! But these people had been out in the field, so they hadn't heard.

Still, the farmer saw a man in an exotic orange suit with a futuristic white helmet, and he did not see an airplane. He raised his pitchfork warily; I thought he might try to run me through!

I pulled up the faceplate on my helmet.

"Did you come from outer space?" he asked.

"Yes, yes, I came from outer space!"

Still he looked suspicious! Perhaps he was thinking of Gary Powers, the U-2 flight that had come crashing to earth not all that long before. Surely he knew that C.I.A. spies can learn perfect Russian! "Who are you?"

"I'm a real man! A Soviet man, a Russian, just like you!" I pointed at the letters over my forehead: C.C.C.P.

Here he finally relaxed a little. The woman had gathered her child to her side; they watched as the farmer helped me gather my parachute. He started talking, babbling excitedly. There were cars coming up on the roadway and I don't remember much of what he said.

I do remember thinking: what now? I need to report in, that's what!

And he started asking about my flight, and I didn't know what I was allowed to say, so I think I told him I needed to find a telephone. (In truth, I think we were both drunk with excitement!)

And now we were walking over to the road. And I'd been up in the parachute for so long, floating down for so long, that people all over the countryside had seen me. So it wasn't long before more people joined us, good people, peasants, sons and daughters of the Soviet soil, all insatiably curious about where I'd been and what I'd seen and what it felt like. And there were more cars on the road now, and men with uniforms getting out, anxious.

"Gather around, gather around!" I told everyone who had helped me. "We need to get some photographs!" As if any of us was going to forget! Still, I wanted a picture. To get everyone together, to say: we are all part of this historic day. Even if we're not all equal participants, we're all a part of it.

But it was not to be. The men in the uniforms had arrived, and they weren't interested in pictures—they wanted to get me out of there and hand me off to the appropriate authorities. (This was the type of thing that could make or break careers for everyone who was even remotely involved.) Seeing two captains, I saluted, but they did the same, anxiously, and there was some awkwardness until they told me what they'd heard on the radio, that I'd been promoted to major. And they shepherded me over to the cars—and they, too, started asking me about my flight! And there was some comic haggling—about whether we should drive to their office in Saratov or to the air base outside Engels, and whether I was to sit in the front of the car or the back, and who would have the privilege of driving me, and so forth. (After a few minutes of this, I even offered to drive. I wasn't entirely joking!)

Then when we were at last rolling away—me in the back of the lead car, the captain still discussing where to go!—a helicopter came swooping out of the sky, the noise of its rotors drowning our conversations and ending the bickering.

In a matter of minutes I was inside it. I looked out the window and saw the peasants still standing there, some waving, some jabbering excitedly; the farmer was pointing out where I'd landed, where he'd seen me, our footsteps through the soil. Our lives had been blown together quite literally by the winds, and now in a blast of rotor wash, we were being propelled apart, and he was now covering his face against the whirlwind of dirt and grass. But even in those few minutes, I'd noticed something in his eyes: a strangeness, a separation. And soon I knew it wasn't going away.

The helicopter flew me to the base outside Engels, where I spoke by phone with Khrushchev himself.

From there I was whisked away to Kuybyshev. And I was being driven to an officers' cottage on the outskirts of town and there were crowds of people in the street already, throngs of people spontaneously celebrating my flight! And our motorcade was hard to miss—a police motorcycle escort and cars full of men in green uniforms and me, still in the blue pressure garment from my spacesuit. And some bystander from the crowd even—quite impulsively!—tried to slide his bicycle under our car tires, to slow us up and get a better look at me! He was willing to wreck his own bicycle and risk police wrath for a few seconds in my presence, a better look, a clearer memory!

I'd known everything was going to be different. That was when I knew it would also be beyond my control.

●●●

But now, at least, everything is back under control.

I'm on my way to the moon, and the first phase of my journey is over, and I have to get used to something I've never had in space: routine. The basics of life—eating and sleeping, and all those other bodily functions one doesn't discuss in polite company. I am a real man, after all.

We are no longer eating from tubes—now there are meal packs. I eat sausages, carrots, and chocolate, then set their empty weightless containers spinning like satellites, like space stations. From my juice pack I take a long pull with the straw, then pull the straw out and squeeze the liquid back out. It hangs suspended, a shimmering yellow globule that quivers in front of me. I stab it with the straw, suck it down a few sizes, and then I make a jerky move and it splits in half. I try to gobble each half up but don't quite get the second. It clings strangely to my face—with no gravity, it doesn't drip off. I root around for a sponge to dry myself.

There are a few things to do after lunch, but not much. Solar radiation measurements. Deployment of the high-gain antenna, which will transmit the television signal back to Earth.

Then we test the television system, which looks not all that different from the one on East-1, although here the technical specifications are better, and there is an additional camera mounted externally. I turn on the lamp that's bolted to the instrument console and squint into its glare. Then I settle back into my couch. I see one of the packages from lunch floating up by the camera and swat it out of the way.

"Let me know if I'm in sight, Dawn-2."

"I see you, Yura!" Blondie says in my ear. "Smile for us."

I give a smile but it feels forced. (There's something in the eyes you can't fake, some emotional energy you transmit involuntarily when you're really and truly happy. And you receive a bit of it, looking at someone else who's truly happy. It seems like something worthy of study, but then again it seems like something you know intuitively already, one of those experiments whose results don't surprise.) The camera's inscrutable eye does not change, does not twinkle to catch the light, does not make me want to smile back. It is a problem with which I am well familiar.

"Good," Blondie says. "Now show us the moon. I'll give you the coordinates."

He reads up the translations in the x, y, and z axes that will get the external camera properly oriented. There is some stickiness to the z-axis translation and it takes a few thrusts back and forth before I'm correctly oriented and I can call it out.

"It's at the right bottom of the frame," Blondie responds, so I make a couple quick pulses with the thrusters and he's happy. Meanwhile I see nothing.

"I'd like to get a look myself," I tell him.

"Very well."

After a quick pulse, I can see the moon in the porthole, half full. Already it is looking bigger. For every other human in recorded history it has been the same size. But not me, not now.

•••

The second day after East-1, they flew me to Moscow.

I had been a nobody, a simple fighter pilot in his late 20s, and now I was descending to the tarmac to report to Khrushchev himself. Such a staged spectacle! Amidst all my smiling and waving on the way down the airplane stairs, I remember thinking how silly it was. As if Khrushchev didn't know the flight was a success! If it hadn't been, I wouldn't have been there.

Still, I felt confident: I had checked myself off in the small mirror of the airplane lavatory, and every time I turned my head I saw the shoulder boards of my new rank, these unfamiliar symbols of the state's approval. But at the bottom of the stairs: catastrophe! I realized my shoelace was untied. Ahead of me lay the red carpet, the dais, the dignitaries and the cameras and Khrushchev himself, and everyone was looking, and there was no way to tie my shoe. For a brief moment I imagined tripping, losing my shoe, or worse, falling on my face in front of the world. Believe me, I was more nervous than I had been orbiting the earth!

But I strode off smartly. Saluted and reported. Nobody else noticed the shoelace, not then. And Khrushchev was obviously elated. Another son of the soil made good.

Then it was time for the motorcade to Red Square. Getting into the car, I at last had time to tie my shoe. We rolled on through the city, past more people than I ever would have imagined. And after that, standing on Lenin's tomb, looking out at the crowd—they seemed genuinely happy. There were immense posters of Lenin, and next to them, posters of me, every bit as large. I smiled and waved. And I thought constantly that I had better not make an ass of myself. And: do I really deserve all of this?

That night, they brought me by the control room of the state television station to review footage of the day's festivities. My untied shoelace was clearly visible.

"We can go ahead and take that footage out, sir," the technician said.

"No. Leave it in. I insist." I figured: let them know I'm a real man.

•••

Another silent meal.

More food packs. This time, veal and cheese. Better than what I had in the isolation chamber, but still, it depresses me. Although I'm the first man to truly voyage out into the solar system, we are not yet capable of living here. Existing for brief periods of time, yes. Eking out a few days in the midst of a vast and all-consuming nothingness. But that's all. No life, in the grand and full sense. Just preventing death. How long will it be before space feels like home? Perhaps it will be different when we have bases on the moon, on Venus, on Mars. Places to go. Beds to lay down on at night.

(It might have been better had this been a two-man voyage. It was supposed to be, originally—as much as I enjoyed being first on East-1, this time I'd wanted someone along for the ride. I'm not a narcissist, after all! Not so eager for triumph that I need to hoard it all for myself. And we were training as a two-man crew—myself as commander and Kubasov as flight engineer. But, of all things, it turned out the designers were having a hard time with the loads for the parachute system, and the burden on the environmental system. And the easiest way to make sure both would work properly was to remove one cosmonaut and launch couch, subtracting a set of lungs and a couple hundred kilograms so as to bring all the equations within the safety margins.)

The 7K-L1 is hurtling moonward, but more slowly now. Second cosmic velocity means I've acquired enough speed to escape Earth's gravity, but it doesn't mean Earth's gravity has no effect on me. So my ship will get slower and slower and slower over the next couple days until I'm in the moon's sphere of influence, at which point I'll start accelerating once more. I cannot feel this—it affects me the same way as it affects my craft, so my body has no motion relative to the walls of the ship. All I know is numbers and readouts. My body floats in weightless oblivion.

I realize that, in my eagerness to get the television testing done, I'd not done a thorough job of cleaning after lunch. The empty package I'd swatted away is now stuck to the intake for the environmental system. I grab it, then see a couple stray bits of food that somehow got loose. It's strange cleaning in space: you can't just assemble a pile of trash. You can take something, some bit of rubbish, and assign it its own airspace and it will stay there, as long as it's not too close to the intakes or outlets for the environmental system. But then if you bump into it, it will go caroming off into some hard-to-reach spot that will force you to bend your arm like a contortionist just to get it, like when something rolls under your bed.

The problem's made worse by the fact that one must take care of all one's bodily functions in this weightless environment, and any errors can result in disgusting little brown specks or yellow globules floating about the cabin along with everything else. (It occurs to me that, for all its fun, weightlessness is also chaotic, whereas gravity at least imposes a certain order on things: unwanted objects fall to the ground and either disappear down drains and sewers, or remain there to be swept up and disposed of in the dustbin.)

When at last all the housekeeping chores are done, I settle in for my sleep period.

One can't call it night, of course, for there's no such thing in cosmic space. And it turns out that one of the nightshades for the portholes is stuck and won't come down. The moon ship must rotate about the solar axis for the bulk of the trip, so there's nothing to be done, no way to keep out the sun.

The sleep periods have been scheduled to coincide with gaps in our transmission coverage. (The relay ships can do in a pinch, but we're trying to rely on land-based stations and Lightning satellites for the bulk of our transmissions at translunar distances.) Given my excitement about the flight, and assorted other household issues, I didn't get a lot of sleep on my last few nights in our apartment in Star City, nor did I get much the night before the launch, since I had to wake up early. I'm tired, and longing for one night of clean full sleep to get caught up.

But: nothing.

I think of Valya, and our children. (Are you judging me now, for taking so long to mention my wife? You shouldn't. On such adventures, it's best not to clutter one's mind with thoughts of home, particularly when there's work to be done.) Valya knew something was up before I left; I couldn't entirely contain my excitement. And of course, in the ways of women everywhere, she took that as an excuse to be petulant and pouty. (Women are of course nervous about things like spaceflight—a judgment born of ignorance. Forgive me. Tereshkova is of course excepted, though she and her ilk are the exceptions that prove the rule.) Although my wife didn't know for sure I'd be going into space, there were enough similarities with the last time that she suspected it. She wants me to be happy with her and the children, at home. She doesn't want me to be off doing dangerous things. (Unless of course I've been home for more days than normal, in which case she wants me out of her hair. Surely this is how it is for everyone! None of this should be foreign to you! Further from the eye, closer to the heart.)

Still nothing. No sleep.

I watch the spot of sunlight from the porthole as it slices a slow circular path across the inside of the ship's hull. Moving in phases: narrow stab wound to slender ellipse, fattening into a circle, then waning and disappearing.

I try again to get comfortable. The problem of the arms is paramount. On their own, they float up, and one gets worried about bumping a switch. And worry, of course, is the thief of sleep. I try to tuck my thumbs under my straps, but then of course there are issues of circulation.

To be a real man means to explore, to test one's limits, to see how far one can get and still make it back home. I would have taken my wife and our daughters with me if it were possible, although of course it isn't, so perhaps this is just an empty wish, wasted words.

I fall asleep.

I wake up.

I fall asleep.

I wake up.

•••

As I said before, everything changed after my flight. I was born again, deposited into a new life; my closest connections were the same, but everything beyond them was not, and even every interaction with them felt different.

And my role was new: I was a representative of the state. When they realized how my flight had captured imaginations, not just in the Soviet Union, but in the world-at-large, they sent me all over. I had never left my country before my flight; now I was going everywhere. A whirlwind tour.

I'm proud to say I handled myself well. For the most part.

In Manchester, when I visited England, it was raining severely. But people had lined up in the streets to see me all the same! (Here and there I was being compared to President Kennedy. It was embarrassing, but I suppose I can see why: we were both young faces for our countries. Proof that we were moving dynamically forward into a better future. Countries need their old faces, too—their Khrushchevs, their Eisenhowers. But people do get bored of the past, and yearn for something new. Youth and hope and strength and vigor. Potential. I did not expect this level of excitement, let me assure you! It was truly humbling, and a reminder of something fundamentally human: the desire for better accomplishments, longer trips, progress: the relentless march away from the dustbin of history and towards a clean and new future.)

The trade union that had sponsored my visit had arranged for a motorcade, a train of black convertibles to take me through the city and give the masses a chance to see me. But they had put the tops up on the cars, because of the rain.

Soon we were inching through the rain-slick streets. I'd seen the crowds at the airport. I didn't expect them elsewhere. But when I wiped the fog from the car's inside windows I saw: they were still there! Lining the roads, despite the awful weather! Crowds of wet people, blurry shapes in the rain—all there to see me!

"Stop the car. Put the top down," I told the driver.

Kamanin gave me a look.

"If they're willing to stand in the rain to see me, I should at least return the favor," I told him with a grin.

And so we rode, open-topped, through Manchester. The people seemed to love it. And Kamanin, in turn, appreciated that.

Still it was bizarre. That was a highlight, but there were many, many more lights. A maelstrom of publicity. The strange dislocation of unexpected trip after unexpected trip. This type of travel produces envy in those who observe it, but anxiety for those who are doing it, those who cannot escape. For I was truly caught in the whirlwind.

• • •

Enough reminiscing. I should focus on the present. It is, at least, more calm.

During this first night there are periods of sleep and wakefulness replacing one another in turn, all while the spacecraft spins about the solar axis. I do my best not to look at the instruments too often; at the beginning of my sleep period, the flywheels of my mind had been spinning at too great a rate, and I certainly don't want to impart them with any additional momentum.

After what feels like a longer bit of sleep, I wake and know I might as well get going. (Well, relatively speaking. In this situation, every function of every bit of furniture is merged into one: my form-fitting couch is bed and workchair and dining room place setting. So there's no place to go, relatively speaking.)

I retrieve the binder with the mission parameters. I compare the counter with the mission-elapsed time to the printed tables and values. It is not quite time for the next communication period, so I eat, slowly, my mind as empty as the vacuum outside the porthole glass.

This evening will be the mid-course correction, which will keep us on track to go around the moon and hit the reentry corridor back at Earth. If there are absolutely no errors, all of that will happen on its own, but I am eager to make sure we're on course.

The reentry is a serious business and I should discuss it in detail now; it's more complicated than the one on East-1, and that one was problematic on its own, so among the mission phases, this one has been foremost in my mind.

Imagine throwing a stone into a pond. If you throw it in directly, there will be a violent splash. But with the right shape of stone, thrown at the right speed and angle, you can skip it and it will slip gently beneath the surface. This is what we're trying to do: at return speeds very close to the second cosmic velocity, there's more energy to be dissipated, and plunging directly into the atmosphere with no letup would make for a difficult time. (It can be done: a ballistic reentry, it's called. But the stresses can be tremendous: at best, it will subject me to 8 to 10 gs. If it's steeper, the deceleration will go up, possibly to 20 gs or more. And the greater strain on the heat shield might even lead to a catastrophic burn-through.) But of course a skip must be a very precise maneuver: a single skip, so as to bleed off exactly the right amount of energy and come back into the atmosphere so as to land at precisely the right spot.

Now imagine throwing the stone, and the pond is small. If you throw very hard, you could easily skip it in such a manner that the stone bounces off the water once and then lands on the opposite bank. And so it is with this. If we don't dig deep enough into the atmosphere on the first skip, the craft will go caroming off into space; it could conceivably end up back in orbit, with no retrorockets and no way to return; it could also end up skipping high and then plunging back down into an unsurvivable ballistic reentry.

We do at least have options for controlling the skip. Thrusters on the descent module can fire to rotate the ship during its reentry; it's shaped like an automobile headlamp, with the heat shield where the front of the lamp would be, and the craft is weighted such that the shield will hit the atmosphere at an angle and either lift the craft up or dig it deeper into the air, depending on the rotation. So there's more to the skip than just hitting the reentry corridor. But we do have to hit it.

Which means tonight's burn is important, not so much for getting to the moon, as for getting back safely. I do not like to dwell negatively on the future. But there is not much else to think about today.

•••

A lot of what I've told you about my past is already in the history books.

I have not talked in detail about the end of East-1 before now, at least not openly. Of course I reported everything in detail to the State Commission. They needed to attempt a fix of the umbilical cord before Titov's mission. But to talk in public about that? At the time it served no purpose. We were first. That's what mattered. There's no use looking sloppy on the world stage.

As for the parachute landing...well, the story is that I came down in my craft. You can blame the Americans for that. When it was becoming apparent we were competing to be first with a man in space, the aeronautical federation that sets the rules for such things was dominated by Americans. And—like children who know they can't win a game fairly— they made sure the rules favored themselves. Those guidelines said that the man who went into space had to land with his craft. And since everyone knew they'd be landing their capsules in water and we'd be recovering ours on land, it was clearly a biased rule, for it's obviously harder to do a soft landing on land. (Not that it really matters. Is someone in Africa or Asia going to say, "No, you cheated, your accomplishment doesn't count" because of such a trifle?)

I knew what was expected of me.

The journalists from the West were eager to talk to me. In England they had arranged a press conference: me behind a table, with microphones and cameras waiting to pounce on any misstep or misstatement. (It was not my first—there had been one in every country—but certainly it was the one with the greatest potential for disaster.) And of course, Kamanin was there in the corner, watching it all. So I could not veer off course in either direction—neither too few words, nor too many.

"Where did your flight begin?" someone asked. (Was it a planted question? Nobody in the West even knew the name Tyura-Tam. To throw off their spies, we'd started referring to the firing range as the Baikonur Cosmodrome, even though Baikonur was hundreds of kilometers away. Surely they wanted to know where to send their spy planes!)

"Where did it begin? At the launch facility," I told them, and there was general laughter.

"After your orbit, you reentered. Where did you land?"

"In the planned spot," I told them. True, we were a few hundred kilometers off course. But everything had gone well. That was the important thing.

"And how did you land?"

"I came down in my craft. Everything functioned perfectly, and I landed, and there were peasants about, and of course they were curious, but the rescue team was on hand very shortly to pick me up." And it was true. I came down in my craft until I ejected. But they didn't need to know that part.

Someone pressed for clarification. "You landed by parachute, or you landed in the spacecraft?" Were they fishing? Did they know the truth? Did they think they could discount my accomplishment based on some absurd rules?

I could feel Kamanin's eyes on my back. I repeated myself: "I came down in my craft."

There was a moment of silence, but too many others had too many other questions. "What was the selection process like? How long before the flight were you picked?" one asked.

"In a timely fashion," I smiled, and the people laughed.

"And do you earn a lot of money as a cosmonaut?" another inquired. "How much do they pay you?"

"Enough!" I smiled, and again they laughed.

So I was perhaps a little reticent to go into details in that setting. And I gave some answers that were perhaps evasive. And it's human nature to assume that someone who is honest in one situation will be honest in another, and that a liar will remain a liar. So are you wondering if you can trust me? You can, I assure you.

•••

The path to the moon already feels like routine. And routine does not make for good stories. But I do want to keep things interesting, and to show you that I can talk about unpleasant things. So I should at least describe my morning urine dump.

I grew up a bit shy when it comes to bodily functions and things of that sort, but when you've been in the company of men, you soon see that they prey on the hesitant and the reticent. So I've gotten used to feigning a certain boldness in such matters. (You may have heard the story that, before East-1, I took a piss on the front wheel of the transfer bus that drove Titov and I to the launch site. As to whether or not it actually happened, you'll have to watch the footage for yourself, but I've stopped contradicting people who tell my story a little differently. And it has become another part of the prelaunch custom, another bit of ceremony for those who want to imitate me. For we are obsessed with ritual in our line of work; when someone wishes you good luck, for instance, you have to immediately say, "Go to hell!") And the urine dump is worth describing. I must say it is one of those absolutely mesmerizing sights: a spray of yellow that crystallizes and sublimates in a few short seconds in the cold vacuum of space, catching the sun's rays gorgeously before it dissipates, grotesque and strangely beautiful and all too fleeting.

And soon, of course, it is back to business. I am maneuvering to photograph the sun's corona. When the portholes are aligned just so, the disc is blocked out and the hazy streaks of light around the edges look fuller and clearer. I shoot picture after picture.

The moon is growing larger, and there's a roundness to it now. The craters show shadows; they're defined in ways I've never seen. My goal has shape and form: it is real.

I look back towards Earth. It's smaller now, perhaps a little bigger than a hockey puck. And yet somehow the distance has made it more beautiful, more alluring; it's clear out here that it's the only thing around. There are three physical components that define every trip: the starting point, the destination, and the space between the two. I'm in that in-between place, and so situated that both starting point and destination look preferable.

"Cedar, this is Dawn-2, Cedar, this is Dawn-2." Blondie's voice. A welcome break in my isolation.

"Dawn-2, this is Cedar. You're looking beautiful down there!"

"Just another day on planet Earth."

"Well, it's nothing to take for granted. If you could see what I see, you'd be a bit more excited."

"Understood, Cedar. Not to dampen your enthusiasm, but the ballistics center believes there is an error in your trajectory. It may have been an alignment issue. We should be able to correct it with our midcourse firing."

"Understood, Dawn-2. How much of a correction?"

"50 meters per second."

"Understood." 50 meters per second: a considerable error.

"We need to do an automatic align with the 100-K to verify that it's working properly."

"Automatic align with the 100-K. Understood." I press the glowing buttons in sequence. The spacecraft swings about.

But there is something amiss. After a longer-than-expected period of cycling, the thrusters stop, and a button flashes on my console.

I consult my binder with the codes and procedures and checklists.

"Dawn-2, this is Cedar. Dawn-2, this is Cedar. Stellar alignment has failed. Stellar alignment has failed." I am not nervous, but I'm hardly pleased. "We were unable to get a lock on Sirius."

"Understood, Cedar. Please confirm with us your filter settings. Also, how long ago was your most recent urine dump?"

"Medium setting for the filters. And the dump was forty-five minutes ago. It seems to have dissipated."

"Some of it may have remained in shadow without sublimating."

"Dawn-2, if it was picking up light and tricking the 100-K, it would start sublimating and disappear."

"It could be the filter, too. Rotate to the lighter one and we'll try again after lunch."

"Understood, Dawn-2."

I eat lunch and then do some housekeeping, and then we give it another go. Still nothing.

Academician Mishin comes on to tell me they are looking through reasons for the alignment failure. The most likely cause is contamination of the optics during launch. But he wants to try again before the midcourse correction.

Once all this is done, I give a quick pulse of the controllers to reorient the craft. I am not sure if Dawn-2 would approve, but they don't have a say in the matter. Now I look out again. The shadows and the phases of the earth and the moon are always opposite of one another when you're travelling between them. My goal is gibbous, waxing, a dead world growing bigger before me, revealing itself to be vaster and more desolate than one could imagine. Meanwhile the little ball of icy blue is waning beautifully, drawing my gaze more than I'd have ever thought.

Blondie has been talking to me about descriptions. Impressions. The colors and shapes of things that are. After East-1, everyone asked me about my flight, and I said it was amazing, and described the colors and shapes and sights. And they could see in my eyes that I had been excited, and they were excited, too. But their excitement was flatter. A reflection. I was excited to have gone into space, and they were excited to be talking to someone who'd been in space.

Telling them how I felt is not the same as getting them to see what I saw. Getting them to feel what I felt.

Blondie is an artist and that's the artist's job, he says. For a simple artist it is to recreate an image. And this is a path to unhappiness. The very best the simple artist can hope for is to create something that looks exactly like the original. And often the simple artist will fall short even of that. For a better artist, he says, the goal is to transform it so it means something. To create an image in a way that also shares a feeling. The yawning mouth of the air lock. The wide eyes of wonder. The smallness of the planet against the emptiness of space.

I unstow the camera and snap several photographs of the earth. If everyone back there could see what I saw...well, surely it would change some thinking. I pay close attention to filter settings, taking comfort in work and artistry. This at least is something I can do well.

•••

I suppose I should talk more about this, in case you don't already know: I do truly love photography. I know—you're probably laughing. I can imagine you thinking: "What does that say? Everyone loves photography. That's like saying you love sunshine." I know, I know. I suppose I should clarify that there are two types of photographers: those who spend time in the darkroom—who put in the effort to learn the chemicals and the master the processes—and pretenders. And I'm no pretender. I don't mean to give offense! It's just that there are levels to these things.

It's funny, of course—I, who love taking pictures, ended up on the other end of the lens more often than anyone. I'm not trying to boast here! If anything, I'm trying to offer some friendly advice, to warn you: be careful of what you love. I don't know if you believe in God or not, and I'll leave it to your imagination how I really feel on such matters, but I suppose I'll say that whatever your beliefs, whether you believe in scientific causes or divine retribution or fate, you should at least appreciate the circularity and the irony of certain things. So be careful of what you love. It will be your undoing.

Perhaps you want to know more about me? I can say this. Venyamin and Alexei, the KGB agents who keep tabs on me during my various appearances: they are my best friends. You might find it sad, or shameful, depending on your beliefs. Then again, you may feel it's patriotically appropriate! Is it because I want them to keep keeping my secrets? Is it a normal human reaction to close proximity over a long period of time in a variety of stressful situations? Is it because I'm simply that innocent and that naïve? You can make of it what you will.

(I will say this: the greatest shrewdness of all is to appear to be innocent. To seem blameless, humble—even ignorant. People are comfortable with that. It may annoy them, but there's some satisfaction in that—it also lets them feel superior, and who doesn't like to feel superior? At any rate, it never threatens.)

My favorite book is actually American. I suppose I can say that now. Hemingway, *The Old Man and the Sea.* Granted, nobody who reads can really have a favorite—it's like asking a person to name their favorite breath of fresh air, or telling a parent to pick their favorite child. Indeed, I'm partial to a lot of books. Jack London, H. G. Wells. And of course Polevoi, *The Story of a Real Man,* which was my introduction to Maresyev. This is the book I always tell people is my favorite. How can you not be impressed with a story like that? Such sacrifice, such courage. Surely everyone of my generation— myself included, of course—must feel humbled by such a hero. And of course it was a handy answer in many conversations. Relatively predictable, certainly nothing that would rock the boat or cause anyone to revise their opinion of me downward. A safe pick. But there's something I love about Hemingway. A real man, too, a hero, and yet not triumphant, for few heroes are. There is struggle everywhere in life, not just in epic battles with fascists, but also in an ordinary battle with a fish. There's struggle everywhere, and nobility in the struggle. (Although perhaps I don't believe that, after all. For if I really believed in the nobility of the ordinary, I would still be in Klushino, tending the soil! I would not have learned to fly, I would not have been the first man in space, I would not now be heading for the moon.)

Still…Hemingway. There's an openness, a space in that book. Something that so many other authors fill in, out of fear you won't understand what they're getting at. With Hemingway there is this space, and the book is like a vessel. You can pour yourself into it and make it yours. That's something Blondie and I talked about, the very first time we met, in fact.

So I've misled people about the end of East-1. And I've even misled people about something as trifling as a favorite book. So, again, perhaps you're wondering how you can believe me now? Well, I'm the only one who can tell this story.

People don't want truth, anyway. They say they do, of course: it sounds good. But what they really want is reliability. Stories are trimmed and sanded and shaped to fit some purpose. Surely they lose some truth in the process. But without that, they are shapeless and without form. And how can something without form have a function?

And of course, this is a type of war, and in war there is deception. During the Great Patriotic War, there were charades on all sides. The British and Americans built fake armies of plywood tanks, used actors playing Churchill and Montgomery to deceive the Germans about their true whereabouts, sent corpses washing ashore with false papers so they'd waste men defending beaches that would never be invaded. Nobody has a problem with such lying, as long as it's done by their side. There is a certain eagerness to see it all revealed at the end, to have someone say, "This, at last, is the truth. It was too dangerous to tell it before, but now it can be revealed." But it's like the thrill of seeing a conjuror's tricks: the early deception is forgiven. And that's what I can say, regarding my earlier evasions: This, at last, is the truth.

•••

My chronometer tells me it's 5:45 p.m. in Moscow—early in the evening of October 27th, 1967. But I'm 246,000 kilometers from Moscow, in a place where absolute time has little meaning, other than as a scheduling convenience. What really matters up here is relative time, mission elapsed time. Man/hours of oxygen consumed, time remaining until reaching the moon, and so forth. And it is at last time for the midcourse firing.

Pavel Popovich was manning the radio for a spell around lunchtime, but now Blondie is back on the control panel. "Well, you haven't made the papers yet, Yura," he says. "White Tass says the English have picked up some transmissions from a Soviet craft headed for the moon. But they're speculating that it's another exercise. Taped transmissions from a mannequin."

I chuckle. "I'm not that boring, am I?"

"I don't think so, but I'm a bit biased."

"If only they knew we're actually talking via radio relay," I say, for the benefit of anonymous Western ears. "I'm back in Star City, transmitting to the spacecraft, which then transmits back to you in Yevpatoriya. It's all an elaborate communications exercise."

Blondie chuckles. "That must be it. You're far too funny to be a mannequin."

(I imagine them listening in: Englishmen and Americans, snooping all over the globe. Am I resentful of their hypocrisy? Or jealous because we don't have their resources? I'll leave that to your imagination.)

"Well, there will be more to talk about anyway, soon enough," I reply.

"We are going to have you try the 100-K again prior to the burn," Blondie says. "If that doesn't work, we'll do a sun-earth alignment."

"Very well."

I strap myself in to the launch couch. It's not like I can get that far away from it—again, the ship isn't all that roomy—but I have been floating during my waking and working hours.

"Confirm you are on the lowest filter setting," Blondie says.

"Confirmed."

The stars are, relatively speaking, fixed in their courses—at least from our perspective. Singular points, far away—exactly what you'd want to use to determine your orientation in three-dimensional space.

Again I press the buttons. Again the spacecraft swings about. Again: nothing.

Since this business started with the 100-K, my unease has been growing. I know I should be on a free-return trajectory, but given the error figure they mentioned, I have my doubts. And even if I am headed back towards Earth, the reentry corridor's just thirteen kilometers wide; at lunar distances, that's rather small, indeed.

But it's also a long way off. We need to do this first.

"We'll go ahead and do a solar align, then," Blondie says.

I page through the binder. A different sequence of buttons: the checklist will keep me straight. I press them in order and the craft swings about. With the sun and the earth and the moon, it's less precise: on such a large body, you need to agree on where you're sighting and taking measurements, or accept a certain level of error. Still, it works.

"Alignment successful," I say.

"And now we will transmit the burn sequence. We will start at mission elapsed time 2 days, 5 hours, 47 minutes. Burn duration: 29 seconds."

I pluck my pencil from the air and write the figures down in the logbook. The burn will happen via ground control, but I need to be prepared to cut off the engine manually.

"I copy 2 days, 5 hours, 47 minutes. 29 seconds of burn. Confirm you will execute on that mark."

"Confirmed."

The timer climbs.

The engine fires and I settle into my couch briefly, but the spacecraft shakes violently. After three seconds, the engine stops.

In my stomach there is a tightness. I force myself to take a deep breath. The worst thing a pilot can do is panic. We will work through this.

"We do not have a full burn. We do not have a full burn."

"Cedar, this is Dawn-2. Confirmed. Incomplete burn." Blondie sounds cool and professional.

"It lasted three seconds, and there was a lot of shaking before the engine shut off."

"Understood. Please check all switch settings, Cedar."

I recheck the lighted pushbuttons to see if some incorrect switch up here could have terminated the burn. But I can't see anything wrong. Everything is as it's supposed to be.

"Dawn-2, Cedar. I have confirmed all my switches. How do you want to proceed?"

There is a delay. Presumably they are conferring. Then: "Cedar, we will attempt another burn in two minutes. Same duration."

The time passes slowly. As the saying goes, there is nothing worse than chasing or waiting. After the interval is up, I ready the stopwatch and the engine fires again. Again comes the vibration. This time it shuts down after two seconds.

"Incomplete burn, incomplete burn," I radio.

The engine, the S5.53, is a simple device. Another hypergolic contraption, with plain valves controlled by redundant electrical relays. There are no ignitors, even. When the valves are opened and the Devil's Venom is mixed, it explodes. There is no logical reason why it should have stopped. But it stopped.

Still, I am confident we can correct our trajectory.

"Dawn-2, this is Cedar, do you have a plan to do another burn?"

A delay. Then: "Sorry, I've been speaking to Mishin. They'll spend the night looking at the data and we'll try a burn tomorrow morning when we're back within relay range," Blondie says. "In the meantime, get some rest and conserve your thrusters."

"Very well."

In the meantime I wait. Again, I am confident. At least, that's what I'm telling myself. There is no point in getting worked up.

I eat dinner in silence. Watching the light move as the spacecraft rotates, it occurs to me that I need to fashion some sort of cover for the broken porthole shade before my next sleep period. And since the first sections of my mission checklist binder—the ones relating to de-orbit procedures prior to leaving Earth orbit—are now useless, I remove those and fold them until I have smallish squares of paper. Then I wedge these impromptu nightshades up against the glass.

I try to fall asleep. Nothing.

I pride myself on my willpower, but sleep is perhaps the area of human endeavor least susceptible to the will. Less than death, even, for that can be hastened through force of will, if one is of that mind. Whereas sleep is the complete absence of will. Then again, there are pills of various sorts...

My thoughts fall apart like nesting dolls. Different parts roll around until they are mismatched. East-1, looking down on the cloud tops from orbit. The Nedelin Incident, tales of inferno, burning men running from an exploding rocket. Sergei Pavlovich's funeral, public recognition at last for the truly indispensable hero of our space efforts, his ashes in the Kremlin wall. Playing on the couch with my daughters. The moment after Foros when I woke up in the hospital, hearing stories of my fall.

I fall asleep.

I wake up.

Is this a dream? No, it can't be. When you are dreaming you don't know you're dreaming, but when you're awake, you know you're awake. And to create confusion between the two is a tactic for a third-rate storyteller, which I am not.

I try not to look at the timer. I tell myself that if I don't see it, I won't worry about how much sleep I have or haven't gotten.

I fall asleep.

I wake up.

•••

You probably haven't heard about the Nedelin Incident. I should perhaps tell you about that in the meantime. It is a state secret, but not as important as it used to be, and it will help you better understand my story.

The story of our country's space triumphs is the story of its strategic rockets. It's this way in America, too, of course—the Atlas that launched John Glenn was a weapon of war, as were the Titans of Gemini. The Americans like to pretend otherwise, to act as if these two purposes of rocketry aren't related! But advances in one turn into successes in the other, just as surely as potential energy is transformed to kinetic.

When Korolev was designing the R-7, Old Number Seven, the goal was to hurl a fusion warhead from one continent to the next. Sergei Pavlovich was working from an early set of specifications from Academician Kurchatov. And because Kurchatov was having a hard time reducing the size of his designs, he was planning on large warheads, so Korolev had to build a large rocket. To get it done quickly he focused on simplicity and reliability. So it was a steel beast, so solid that the technicians could walk around on it when it was lying on its side being assembled. (Quite unlike the elegantly engineered American rockets—so thinly designed that they crumple unless they're full of fuel!)

Because Korolev had to design to such robust specifications, he realized he'd be able to do other things with Old Number Seven. Things he'd been dreaming of for years. Launching satellites, and people. And because he was succeeding with his strategic rocket testing, he was allowed to do these other things. The currency of bureaucracy: not just funding, but decrees and permissions, and successes, which make those who issued the decrees look good, which leads in turn to more decrees and more permissions.

So it all started with strategic rockets. Stalin knew what the fascists had done with rockets, and he knew what was possible, and though he died in 1953, he had set it all in motion.

And we had great successes, indeed! While I was off in Saratov learning to fly, and later passing lonely hours patrolling near the Arctic Circle, Korolev was building rockets for the state. He gave them the means to destroy London, and then New York, so they gave him permission to put a satellite in space. ("If the main task doesn't suffer, then do it," Khrushchev had said.) And because that was such a propaganda coup, they let Korolev put a man in space.

But there was a problem with Korolev's strategic rockets. They worked as promised, but because they were fueled with liquid oxygen and kerosene, they could not be launched quickly, nor could they stay in an advanced state of readiness for very long. Liquid oxygen boils off swiftly, so it must be pumped in during the hours before launch. But Korolev was fixated on using it, and his bureau suffered because of it. (Engineers gather data, of course, but design is also a matter of emotion. Everyone has their preferences and their aversions, and those can lead them down the wrong path for quite a ways, especially when getting started on a project.)

In engineering, as in parenting, changes in direction often take place from generation to generation. In your family, you see the things you didn't like about how your parents raised you, and you do things differently with your children; you may make mistakes, but they're yours, and you've avoided the problems of the past generation. Then your children can choose to go in yet another direction. So, too, with design. Others like Chelomey (and Yangel, who had worked under Korolev but had started his own bureau in 1954) did not have the same biases as Korolev. So for the next generation, they started developing rockets based on hypergolics: chemicals with a high boiling point that could be stored for much longer periods. These chemicals have their own issues; they're corrosive and toxic, to the point that Korolev had started referring to them as "Devil's Venom." But for purposes of strategic rocketry, they're far superior: if your rockets take an hour to launch, and the other side's rockets take a day, you can destroy them at leisure and win a nuclear war without taking too many casualties.

(I should emphasize that none of us wanted such a war! We were survivors, after all, of the most destructive portion of the greatest war in human history. But surely the best way to prevent a war is to convince your opponent you can win one, and the second best way—almost as good—is to convince him he will face unendurable pain if he wins.)

So in 1960, the rush was on to develop and test this new generation of rockets. Yangel's R-16 was the leading contender, and Marshal Nedelin was leading the development program. And of course there was pressure to get things done by the anniversary of the October Revolution.

Rocket testing is a demanding enterprise—long days out on the firing range inspecting components, watching technicians remove panels and replace parts, testing electrical systems and subsystems, developing fueling procedures. And failures have a cascading effect: a circuit fails, a hard-to-reach component must be replaced, a test is delayed, another test cannot take place. And there are other tests—humans, too, are put to the test; tempers flare; decisions must be made to delay or take shortcuts. And Nedelin was a good military man. And those of us in the military know that plans must be executed on time, and for that one must sometimes take shortcuts.

The rocket was put out on the pad on the 23rd of October, and it was fueled and was being made ready, but there was a problem with a sequencer. And the safe thing would have been to drain the rocket. But the safe thing is never the shortcut. The State Commission decided to make repairs without draining it, and Nedelin concurred. And the next day, while the launch complex was still full of people, the engines of the second stage ignited.

(The survivors and witnesses were strictly forbidden to discuss the incident. But Sergei Pavlovich knew the rough magnitude of the disaster as soon as it happened, and he heard details from the survivors afterwards: the official reports, and the drunken late-night stories of horror and remorse. And not long before his death, Korolev, in turn, got drunk at a party and told me.)

The engines ignited with a roar that every survivor described as the most unexpected and frightening sound they'd ever heard. Within seconds, the second-stage engines had burned through the first stage's propellant tanks. And these exploded in a hellish inferno, a bright brown-yellow cloud and a tower of flame.

The images from this must have been truly horrifying, for they remained clear in the retelling, from others to Korolev, from Korolev to me: burning people running from the pad before succumbing to the toxic fumes, and others shattering legs and backs jumping from concrete landings to escape the inferno.

Nedelin was dead. So, too, were many others. Some were disintegrated, or burned into piles of ash; Nedelin's remains were only identified by the remnants of the medals on his uniform. Even years later when he told me the story, Korolev did not know the final tally, but he had heard some numbers: 74, and 78, and 126.

Yangel had survived. He'd survived by the slimmest of chances; he'd survived because of a cigarette.

Nedelin's deputy Myrkin wanted to quit smoking, and he'd decided that that day, October 24th, would be his last cigarette. So he'd wanted one final smoke break a half hour before launch. And of course all smokers want someone to smoke with, so he'd grabbed Yangel, and they'd gone into one of the concrete blockhouses to smoke.

I do not know all the details of Yangel's actions; we were never close, so he never told me, and anyhow only the worst sort of person goes about asking another human being to describe the worst day of their life. But I imagine it here and there: Yangel in the blockhouse, hearing the noise, his heart instantly racing—he surely knew what was happening. And the normal human impulse is to help, so he and Myrkin surely could have rushed instantly out of the blockhouse, but I imagine Yangel was too smart to do that; I imagine him waiting at least a few minutes, until the flames had burned down and the fumes from the hypergolics had dissipated. So perhaps they just raced to the viewing slits to see it; perhaps they saw the rocket topple and explode, all their plans turning to catastrophe. And that's how I imagine it—Yangel at the viewing slit, looking out at the running burning people, standing in helpless horror. (Not that I blame him! I might well have done the same. I only know that in such situations, one wonders endlessly whether one has done everything possible, and even if the answer is "Yes," one feels guilty afterwards. I'm glad I wasn't faced with that choice!) I keep imagining. This is the power of such events, and the stories they spawn—they stay alive in your imagination, in your dreams; you create your own visions and scenes.

Afterwards, Khrushchev appointed Brezhnev to head the commission to investigate the catastrophe. And it might surprise you to know, depending on your perceptions and prejudices about our country, but Brezhnev insisted that there be no punishments. Investigations and answers, yes, but no punishments. The guilty, Brezhnev said, have already been punished.

The moral of the story, as far as the state was concerned, was to drain rockets during such work, and to install safeguard circuits to prevent spurious signals from igniting the engines before launch. Myrkin reportedly drew an additional lesson: don't ever stop smoking, because it might save your life. And I came to my own conclusion when I learned that the cottage in which Titov and I slept the night before East-1, the little white cottage that everyone referred to as "Korolev's cottage" had, in fact, been Nedelin's cottage before his death. So much for lucky rituals.

Yangel had been hoping to take a leading role in rocketry, but after that he was busy making up lost ground and getting the R-16 deployed in a timely fashion. Chelomey's bureau ultimately gained on both Yangel and Korolev, at least for a while; Chelomey was developing his own hypergolic strategic rockets. (And of course he had hired Khrushchev's son, which certainly didn't hurt, at least not until Khrushchev was deposed.) There are of course no needles or indicators or gauges for such things, but everyone can sense how power shifts from one design bureau to others in the wake of such calamities. OKB-586 loses, OKB-1 holds steady, OKB-52 gains. New decrees, new directives, and funds and people to go with. And no one wants to stand in the way of a decree.

As for Nedelin, there was no mention of the catastrophe in our press. Just a brief story, a single sentence: "Marshal Mitrofan Ivanovich Nedelin, 57, Chief of Strategic Rockets, died in a plane crash in an undisclosed location."

Why am I sharing this with you? Chelomey's period of advance allowed him to develop the Proton, of course, which gave him a part in this mission, but there's more to it than that. I bring it up because it's indicative of the way we have done things. For unlike the Americans, we don't go blathering away about every mistake, every misstep. We have launched probes to Venus and Mars; we do not announce them when they fail in their assigned objectives. If they fail, they get innocuous names—Cosmos, and a number—and only if they succeed do they get a name indicative of their mission. There is no need to look foolish.

There have been some secondary effects to these tendencies, of course, just as there are unintended additional consequences to every course of action. Our discretion regarding launch failures has spawned rumors regarding our space program, absurd stories that would perhaps not otherwise exist. On my travels, I've heard fanciful tales of lost cosmonauts, people like Ilyushin's son who were supposedly launched before me but then failed to come back successfully, and who were consequently never discussed because such stories would embarrass the state. I know how ridiculous these stories are! But can I convince anyone else? Of course not. In their mind, I have an interest in maintaining the deception.

Still, I'm proud of our judgment and discretion in such matters, especially regarding something like the Nedelin catastrophe, with such obvious implications for our nation's security. Can anyone who survived the Great Patriotic War think ill of such behavior? We face a new enemy, an enemy of tremendous resources, tremendous strength. And against such an enemy, one must also appear strong, just as animals puff themselves up to dissuade aggressors. It's natural to do what we've done! And so we held May Day parades with rows of rockets rolling through Red Square and Khrushchev looking on, and soldiers driving those same rockets down the side streets and around and back to parade them through Red Square again, to make us look stronger, as if we could build an unending succession of rockets. And flights of bombers flying over, then taking a loop around the outer city and getting in line to fly over again. A conveyor belt of military hardware. The illusion of infinite strength. And no mention of failures and catastrophes, particularly regarding the development of strategic rockets. So we have lied, perhaps, but these are lies that prevent war. Surely there is nobility in such lies!

•••

In my morning I pull my makeshift paper cover from the broken porthole and raise the shade on the other one. Sunlight scrapes my tired eyes. I barely eat.

Even now, I am not yet at the moon. Today is the last full day of the trip there, and it promises to be a day of troubleshooting the engine failure. As always in these situations, we must determine the answers to the three key questions: What went wrong? Who is to blame? And (most importantly): What do we do now?

"Good morning, Cedar," Blondie says, somewhat crackly. "How did you sleep?"

"Not well, Blondie."

There is a delay. For a moment I wonder if it's a problem with the transmitter, on top of everything else. Then I remember: at these distances, it takes time for our words to travel. More than anything, this tells me how great a void lies between me and home: even the radio waves cannot sprint across it.

Then at last: "Ahh, yes. If it makes you feel any better, the engineers haven't slept at all. So compared to them, you're well-rested."

"Yes. And it's a bright and sunny day, at least. Not a cloud in the sky." I'm tired enough that this seems funny in my mind. But out loud it falls flat.

"That's the spirit," he says at last.

"What do we know so far?"

A wait, then: "The alignment issue and the engine problem appear to be unrelated. As we discussed, the 100-K..." (His voice crackles.) "...failing in stellar alignment mode due to optical contamination issues discussed yesterday. As for the engine..." (Crackles.) "...analyzed the firing data. It appears the engine is shutting off the fuel flow due to..." (There is a final blizzard of static.)

"Dawn-2, this is Cedar. Say again your last."

I breathe. I wait. For my fate, or just instructions on what to do next.

"Yura, the engine is shutting off its own fuel flow due to low pressure readings in the combustion chamber."

"Understood. Low pressure readings. Do we know why?"

Again I wait.

Another voice. Mishin: "The shutdown is by design, Yuri. To prevent flooding the engine with fuel if the engine is defective. You could have a manufacturing defect in the combustion chamber which is preventing normal firing of the engine."

"Could it be a faulty sensor?"

I scan the instruments before they reply. Then: "It is possible, Yuri. We will try again manually, but if it doesn't work, we will need another plan."

"Understood. Please let me know the parameters of my burn."

A pause. If nothing else, the transmission delays are forcing an extra level of calmness into our conversation. "We will attempt a burn in fifteen minutes. We'll have you do a solar alignment beforehand. Start time for the burn: Mission elapsed time of 3 days, 2 hours, 37 minutes. Burn duration: 31 seconds."

I pluck my pencil from the air and copy everything down. Then I repeat it: "I have: 3 days, 2 hours, 37 minutes mission elapsed time, manual burn duration of 31 seconds." These are the things you write down, the things you double- and triple-check.

"Good luck, Yura," Blondie says.

"Go to hell, Blondie."

I strap myself back in. Run through the alignment procedures again.

When at last it is time for the burn, I watch the seconds count down. I bring my hand up to the panel five seconds early, as if it might get delayed along the way.

I stab the button. Nothing.

"We do not have a burn," I transmit. "We do not have a burn."

Now there is a delay not caused by the distance alone, but by the gravity of the situation. "No burn." Blondie says at last. "Understood, Cedar." And there is another delay and a muffled conversation and he comes back on. "We're going to walk back through the switches and attempt it again. Please reset everything to the initial settings. We will attempt it again at 3 days, 2 hours, 43 minutes. Burn duration still 31 seconds."

Again the countdown. Again I press the button, harder this time. Again, nothing.

As I wait for an answer, I should point out that I've spent time down there during such crises, so I know the techniques we use. There are six rules, which might serve you well:

1) Calm discussions only. (Order and reason will solve our problems. Chaos is the enemy. And few things are more chaotic than a noisy discussion among intelligent people who are proud of their intelligence.)

2) Everyone is guilty until they prove themselves innocent. (There are many possible reasons for failure, and the tendency is to point fingers. Which is acceptable here, because it's best to cast a wide net when looking for the causes of problems in complicated systems. So if you are responsible for a system, or a part, it is up to you to prove that it didn't cause problems with the whole.)

3) Between larger meetings, everyone will work in a small group with a specific task—studying telemetry, for instance, or getting answers about factory testing procedures, or looking at design drawings.

4) Any hypotheses must be tested at the factory using the next spacecraft awaiting flight to see if the problem can be reproduced.

5) Members not under suspicion must not busy themselves with observing these discussions, but must continue to provide normal flight support for the craft.

6) A group must also be formed to start writing up the findings of the various committees.

So I can almost picture everyone at Yevpatoriya: tense, poring over schematics and memos, choking on the bitterness of yesterday's wrong decisions, or savoring the thin satisfaction of someone else's mistakes.

At last, Blondie's back. "Yura, Mishin believes there may be a problem with the fuel tank integrity because of the vibrations during the failed firing." We both know what all of this means. The fuel is gone. So regardless of the cause of the vibrations, the engine is now useless. "We are going to have to work out an alternate plan."

Popovich comes on around lunchtime so Blondie can get a break. He is ordinarily a jovial man, but there is a hesitancy now. Nobody quite knows what to say to someone in my situation.

I am doing some housekeeping and getting the cabin straight after lunch when Mishin breaks in. Even he is quieter and more circumspect now.

"How is my trajectory?" I ask.

"We will know more once you round the moon tomorrow. Given the mass concentrations, there is some uncertainty. But we believe you are currently not on track for a free return."

This is serious. They think I will miss Earth on my way home. I will round the moon and come back towards it, but I will not reenter the atmosphere, and the earth will sling me off into some new direction.

Mishin and I both know he is no Sergei Pavlovich. In fact, we've had heated words in the past. But now all that feels far away. In the midst of such seriousness, all personal feuds seem temporary, insignificant. We are united in shared crisis.

"Understood," I say.

"We are working on an alternate course of action," he says. "We will have more details tomorrow."

I don't know if he has a serious and credible plan, or if he is just telling me what he thinks I want to hear.

"Understood," I repeat.

I am exhausted. I eat a few packages for dinner—chicken and potato paste. I clean up and take care of my business and turn off the interior lights.

I fall asleep. A deep, hard, heavy sleep.

•••

I wake up.

In the night I've had dreams I barely remember, dreams about the war.

We suffered greatly back then, of course. And like all great tragedies, it has given all of us who survived it a sense of identity and purpose and meaning. I used to think it was a sign of particular national greatness that we had gone, in the course of two decades, from having fascists at the gates of our capital, to launching a man into space. And I am still proud, but now I understand the sadness beneath it: when you have gone through such misery on Earth, you are going to try all the harder to escape. The Americans are fat and full; they do not have the same urgency to go elsewhere.

In my dream we had been occupied again. It was one of those dreams where you somehow know and accept certain facts which don't make logical sense. I was still me, still in my 30s, still a cosmonaut, but we had been occupied by the Germans. An awful, helpless feeling. After such dreams, I am always grateful to wake up. Even now, in a crippled spacecraft, on a mission whose outcome seems dubious, life feels preferable to those dark days.

My family spent the war living in an earthen dugout in our backyard because the fascists had kicked us out of our home.

Only by watching the skies could I imagine freedom: the brave Soviet pilots doing battle above always gave us hope. But life on the ground was hell. I saw the fascists hang my brother to within an inch of his life.

Even this uncertain trip feels better than that. And I am well-rested, for the first time all mission. Sleep makes all the difference. One's situation doesn't change, but one's attitude does.

I enjoy my morning meal. Whatever else happens, today I am going to be the first man to go around the moon. Nothing is going to stop that. Everything else may be in doubt, but this is certain.

The ship is travelling faster now. We're close enough to the moon that its gravity reigns supreme. Earth's pull is ineffectual.

I'm putting away my empty breakfast containers when I glance out the window and see a thick swath of grey and tan, mottled craters and mountain shadows and the smoother dark lowlands, the *mare*, what old Italians thought were lunar seas. I unstow the camera and snap frame after frame.

We are approaching along the darkened side, so beneath the shrinking bright stretch of moon there is a vast void yawning, a dead space lit dimly blue with earthlight. And my arms go to gooseflesh. I am really at the moon, and it is impossibly huge and round and real, and so close that it's blocking out a large segment of my field of view. I stretch to watch for as long as possible while the spacecraft continues its solar roll. This is truly something.

"Cedar, this is Dawn-2." Blondie's on again. I calculate it out, and I can tell he's working far longer than the normal shift, even with the middle breaks.

"Dawn-2, this is Cedar. Are you in trouble, Blondie?"

"No, why do you ask?"

"They certainly have you working long hours."

"I'm in trouble with myself, Yura. I'm punishing myself. I don't want to miss this, though. Not for the whole world."

"Neither do I." A pang in my heart. If we cannot correct my trajectory, I am perhaps going to miss the whole world for this. Is it worth it? Who can say?

"We have the estimated communications blackout time, Yura. It will begin at 12:34 Moscow time. 3 days, 6 hours, 31 minutes total mission time. It should last 47 minutes."

"Very well." We will, of course, be out of radio contact as I round the moon. A different kind of loneliness than anyone's ever experienced. "It's quite the sight so far. I'm sure I'll have plenty of descriptions when I come back around. Do we have a start time for the broadcast?"

And now there is another long delay, long enough that my transmission probably had time to go to Mars. "Yura, the State Commission met to discuss your situation following the rocket failure yesterday. Kamanin insisted that there will be no live broadcast."

"Understood, Blondie." Kamanin. I could feign outrage, but I'm not entirely surprised. My situation puts everyone involved in a difficult spot. And there are plenty of times, after all, where Kamanin and I are of the same mind. So this is just another piece of information. Something that's no longer on my task list.

Now the slice of sunlit moon has disappeared completely. I pass into shadow and the light streaming through the porthole cuts off abruptly. But I want to make it darker still, so I cut the interior lights. Now there is only the soft glow of the pushbutton panel and the melancholy yellow of the voltmeter. And outside, all the stars, and beneath them the last earthlit piece of moon is giving way to an immense emptiness, like when flying over water at night. And yet this is unlike anything any human being has ever experienced. How is it that I have been chosen, not once but twice, to be the first man to do such monumental things? It is amazing to be so unique, so alone. And yet I would be a stingy man indeed if I didn't want everyone to see what I'm seeing and feel what I'm feeling.

"It's all dark below me now, Blondie. There's not much to photograph, but finally this is a scene I could paint as well as you."

There's a delayed chuckle, like he's slow getting the joke. (Which he is, of course, but through no fault of his own.) And: "Very good, Yura."

Then it's back to business for the final minutes before we lose contact. Recording cabin temperature and pressure in the logbook, and monitoring voltage and amperage and the performance of the buffer batteries now that the solar panels have nothing to do. Listening to my friend until the radio signal cuts out.

● ● ●

I was in the control room for Sunrise-2, two years ago. There was some doubt about the outcome there as well, so I know how Blondie must be feeling.

After so many public successes—at least in the area of human spaceflight—our leaders became addicted to triumph. And they knew the Gemini program was starting soon, and they knew Union wouldn't be ready for some time, so they stretched the capabilities of the East spacecraft far past its safe limits. That's what the Sunrise spacecraft really were—the same as East, with a different name! I can tell you that now, at least.

With Sunrise-1, they realized that they could cram three men in a capsule originally sized for one, provided nobody wore a pressure suit. It was dangerous, it was reckless, and there was much unpleasant deliberation by the State Commission. But it worked.

For Sunrise-2, they realized that they could build a collapsible rubberized airlock—an inflatable airlock—and mount it *outside* the craft, and have one cosmonaut use it to exit the ship and float freely in space. Objectively speaking (I can say this now!) this was beyond reckless. The Americans had designed their spacecraft to open up in space and allow their men to enter and exit safely. We had made no such provisions.

But of course in our profession, nobody wants to be second. And if you fret too much, they will find someone else, someone better at hiding their fears.

Blondie was selected for this mission. Like me, he was personally chosen by Korolev. Pavel Belayev was flying the spacecraft, but Blondie was the one chosen to walk in space. He had gone through a rigorous training regimen of calisthenics and parachute jumps and weightless trips in the Tupolevs to practice opening the hatches.

When he went into the airlock, everything was going according to plan. There was a television camera mounted outside the ship, and they did a live broadcast on state television of the historic adventure. Everyone could see him floating free, an umbilical cord connecting him back to the ship, his face hidden behind the smooth glassy visor. And, of course, the large letters on his helmet: C.C.C.P. A man in a puffed-up spacesuit swimming above a sea of clouds.

But the puffed-up spacesuit was not part of the plan.

There are always unforeseen effects when doing something for the first time. Blondie's spacesuit had swollen in the vacuum of space, but of course Blondie was the same size, so his fingers were no longer in the gloves. And he needed to grab on to handles, to pull and manipulate himself to get back to the craft, but he could only move with the greatest of exertion. His breathing grew extremely labored; he nearly passed out from the effort.

I was in the control room, monitoring all this. We knew he had to get back inside on his own. There were no provisions for the spacecraft commander to come out and rescue him. If Blondie hadn't been able to get back in the airlock *and* back in the craft, Belayev would have eventually had to cut him loose so as to survive the reentry.

We cut the camera feed to the state television network and told them we were having technical difficulties. Nobody wanted to air his death on television.

When Blondie tried to climb back inside the airlock, he seemed to be having a hard time getting back in.

"Wait one minute," he told us.

We knew something else was wrong. We didn't know what it was. As it turned out, his suit was too wide, now that it had expanded. He was letting air out of his own spacesuit so he could fit back in the airlock. He had to reduce the pressure all the way down to .27 atmospheres. He didn't tell us what he was doing, though! He didn't want us to worry.

Finally he squeezed inside, head first, which was backwards. He had to laboriously turn around inside the airlock to get back inside the ship itself.

State television, I found out later, had cut to somber music. Mozart's "Requiem." The same piece they play when a prominent national figure is dead and they are waiting on a public announcement.

And it turned out the troubles were not over for Blondie and Belayev. They still needed to reenter, but they were having difficulties orienting their craft. The automatic system wasn't working. They had to orient themselves manually and fire the retrorockets on their own.

Seconds make a tremendous difference when you're travelling at first cosmic velocity. They had to perform the manual orientation while unseated, then scramble back into their couches for the retrorocket firing. So they were a few seconds off in timing their burn, and they came down far off course. Their capsule landed in a snowy forest in the Urals, wedged between two trees. The hatch blew open, and it was freezing, and the snow was two meters deep, and Blondie's spacesuit was filled with sweat, all the way up to his knees.

For hours, our rescue helicopters had no idea where they were.

Blondie and Belayev had to spend the night in the capsule, warding off wolves, using the parachute to stay warm.

Finally the next day the rescue helicopters arrived, and they were flown to safety. State television was able to announce the successful conclusion of Sunrise-2. The crisis was forgotten, unmentioned in public. No one was the wiser.

That was our last flight before my voyage to the moon.

• • •

The sun rises again over a bleak panorama, stark and beautiful, sharp in a way earthly landscapes can never be.

I am the first human to see a sunrise over the moon. It is every bit as abrupt as its opposite had been—more so, for the interior lights are still off. I am more alone than any human in history.

I am flying just over 1200 kilometers above an alien world. One of our earliest probes photographed the far side back in 1959, but as usual the real scene's incredibly more detailed. There are more craters than I can comprehend, small ones barely visible and large ones sending streaks for hundreds of kilometers. And none of the smooth dark *mare*—there are some darker and lighter areas, but far less variety of appearance than one sees from the earth, even. Still, it's mesmerizing, like the sea on a sunny windy day. Themes repeating, a common pattern copied endlessly with infinite small variations. For a few precious moments, everything falls away—my uneven past and my uncertain future are now both as remote and invisible as Earth. The only thing real is this unreal scene, and I am alive and aware in a way that I'm struggling to put into words. An exalted feeling of pure existence. Living in the grandest possible sense.

I do have scientific observations to make—I'm looking for volcanoes. It was not the first priority during my training; I only had time for a few hasty hours of instruction crammed into 12- and 14- and 16-hour workdays. But I want to discover something and pass it on. I have to do more than just being here.

The camera is floating next to me. I reload it and start snapping away again, shooting pictures of sharply shadowed holes in countless shades of gray. Flying over the earth, one sees that land is so often shaped by water: folds assemble into ravines, which open into valleys as streambeds accumulate to make rivers. But here of course there are no such processes. And I can't see any volcanoes. Only countless impact craters, holes on top of holes on top of holes, old deep craters whose outlines are disrupted by newer and sharper and smaller craters. A sphere covered with circles and sections of circles. A mottled and pitted surface, like an old cannonball somehow turned from rusty iron to dusty stone.

I have been floating, nose pressed against the glass. We are still rolling slowly, so after a while I must switch to the other porthole. Once I've snapped two more rolls of film, I snatch up my logbook and make a few notes. (I have to work under the assumption I'll get home to deliver these, that all my efforts mean something.) Then I drop the camera and stare, really concentrate on the scene in front of me, the sunlit highlights of innumerable circles. However long I live, I want to remember this as sharply as I see it now.

After a few minutes, I look back at the panel. The timer tells me my communications blackout should soon be over. I settle back into my couch.

"Dawn-2, this is Cedar, come in."

Nothing.

"Dawn-2, this is Cedar."

The radio crackles. "...edar, I am glad to hear you."

"Dawn-2, we are coming back around. All environmental systems nominal. The buffer batteries worked as expected."

"Understood, Cedar. How's the view?"

"You won't need many colored pencils when you're up here, Blondie."

Another delay. He doesn't get the joke. "Please repeat your last, Yura."

"You won't need many colored pencils! Black, grey, white. Maybe tan. You can save weight and leave the rest at home."

"Can you see us, Yura?"

There is another pang—I realize I may have missed the earth rising over the moon! I strain at the porthole closest to the horizon; it's still low, but at the edge of the porthole, so I give a quick guilty pulse of the thrusters to bring it into full view.

Such a magnificent sight!

I want to just stay there and watch, but I know this is too good a picture to miss, and this will be my only chance to get it. And I know even before I look through the viewfinder that this will be a perfect picture, perhaps the best I can ever hope to take. There's something most people don't get about photographic composition. God loves trinity, as the saying goes, and it holds for photographs, too: forefront, middle, backdrop. If you see something magnificent but don't have anything in the scene to give it perspective, it looks far flatter when it's photographed. But here is everything a good picture needs: a dead foreground, a living backdrop, and the vast space between. The earth is blue and white and green, all streaks and swirls, and vibrantly colorful behind the monochromatic moonscape; although the distance is great, it looks as detailed as an object in one's hand. And I feel a swelling in my heart thinking that everyone I've ever met, and everyone I ever will meet, is all the way back there.

I take picture after picture. I know that even a well-composed shot cannot fully capture this feeling, but I know they will be magnificent photographs all the same. And I can imagine people asking me about them, and me saying, "Ahh, yes, but of course, you don't see what's outside the frame. Imagine seeing this, so small, but the only thing with any real color in this vast empty space!"

"Are you still there, Yura?" Blondie asks, but with humor, for he knows the answer.

"This is the most incredible sight. Earth above the moon. I've never seen anything like it, Blondie."

"I talked to Kamanin. He gave permission for you to record a brief message. We still cannot do a live broadcast, of course, but we can at least do this. The State Commission can decide what to do with it later."

"Understood." I am indescribably grateful.

It occurs to me that he could have lied and told me it was a live transmission. But he has been true. Then again, I expect nothing less of Blondie.

"Let me know when you're ready," he says.

I turn on the light and activate the camera. Stare at the smooth slick eye. "I am ready to transmit, Blondie."

"One moment," he says, then: "You are looking good. We are ready to receive your transmission."

I smile. "Greetings fellow Soviet citizens and peace-loving people of all mankind. I am speaking to you from hundreds of thousands of kilometers away after becoming the first man to fly around the moon. I am incredibly grateful to once again represent the Soviet people, and indeed all mankind, on a bold feat of exploration. And I'm particularly humbled by all the hard work of many thousands that made this possible—the wisdom of our Chief Designer, the helpful guidance of his many able deputies, and the skilled labor of many more working under their direction. The legacy of our forefathers, of Marx and Lenin, is a legacy of untiring effort and unlimited progress, and an endless expansion of human potential. I know they'd be proud to see the hammer and sickle rounding the moon, to know that the workers and peasants have triumphed again, and that the first manned spacecraft to go here was piloted by a real Soviet man."

"From here I can see the whole planet, as small as a child's ball. I don't know if I can give you a view, but I hope to bring some pictures back so you all can see what I see. It is not like on Earth where distant things appear blurry: here there is of course no atmosphere, so everything is sharp and clear. I am grateful beyond words to have this perspective, to see things so clearly. For I can see no national boundaries, no distinctions. The only ones that exist are the ones in our mind, the artificial ones created by those who want to rob and plunder and oppress and divide." (Perhaps I am thinking of the Americans here, and their war in Vietnam.) "Like many of us, I survived the Great Patriotic War, and I saw the hellish destruction these decisions can lead to. But when we get away from that, we can see that our planet is truly a beautiful place. It is my deepest hope that one day everyone can see that there are no divisions, and that all the peoples of Earth can join together in peace and prosperity to advance the cause of human potential."

I can't think of anything more to say, and I don't want to start babbling, so I stop and turn the camera off. To Blondie I speak: "Did you get all of that?"

I wait.

And at last, his voice: "Yes, Yura. It was perfect."

•••

Because I need to conserve the thrusters, I do not turn the moon ship to get a better view after we have flown past. I do not see the moon growing smaller behind me.

I suppose it's normal after leaving some monumental destination to want to turn and look back, particularly if you're far from home; I suppose it's even more normal when you know you'll never be back. (Surely you've observed this in your own life! I don't have to know you to know that.)

So there's a pang as I see the lunar horizon slip past the portholes. But we might need the thrusters to get home. Ordinarily they're only for rotations. But we can use them for translations, changing velocity. If we fire them for long enough, we might be able to correct enough of our velocity error so as to make it home safely.

"Dawn-2, come in. Dawn-2, this is Cedar, come in."

"Cedar, this is Dawn-2." Komarov's voice.

"Old man Komarov!" He's only seven years older than me, but that put him at the upper end of our cosmonaut class. He's a veteran of Sunrise-1, a sharp engineer, talented and smart. "What happened to Blondie? I thought he'd be coming back on."

"They ordered him off the console to get some rest, Yuri."

"Very well." I miss Blondie, but I'm glad they're making him take a break. (We all have a tendency to drive ourselves too hard in this line of work, to get by with few breaks until we ourselves are at the breaking point. So when you make someone like Blondie take a break, you are doing him a favor, because he won't let himself have one otherwise.)

"What can we help you with, Cedar?"

"Dawn-2, I want to know if there's a plan to use the thrusters for the midcourse correction."

"I'm glad you mentioned that, Cedar. We were discussing that while you were having your fun."

I chuckle. "Were you going to tell me?"

He laughs. "Everything in its proper time, Yura."

Now I laugh a little. My spirits are good. They will figure out how to get me home. I'm looking forward to seeing my friends, looking forward to the parties and the fun—getting drunk, perhaps, yes, but more than that, the comradeship. And surely they will marvel at the photos I've taken; they will be amazed to see the earth as I have seen it, as it truly is, a precious sparkling gemstone against a dead backdrop of black and white and gray and tan.

Komarov comes back on: "In all seriousness, the ballistics center has been monitoring your trajectory to see how the moon's mass concentrations may have affected it. But once that's in hand and they've run the numbers, we should be able to do a series of thruster firings tomorrow. In the meantime, have some dinner and get some sleep."

"Will do, my friend."

•••

Mathematically, every orbital path can be described as a section of a cone.

Say, for instance, you have a simple cone pointing downwards. If you slice it horizontally, you have a circle. (Slice further up or down the cone, and you will of course have circles of different sizes.)

If you slice at an angle, you'll have an ellipse, provided your slice passes through the central vertical axis of the cone, and at an angle less than the side of the cone. The ellipse may be extremely elongated, but it will be a closed loop; it will begin and end in the same spot. The small end of the cone is like the body you're orbiting; the orbital path will be fast and quick in that tight section, and slow and lazy in the farther reaches. (This is what we're doing with our Lightning satellites, for instance, which spend the long slow period over our territory, where they can transmit for long portions of the workday. And then they zip around while the sun is down and take their place again the next day.)

Now say you take a slice of the cone that doesn't pass through the central vertical axis. Since the cone is open-ended, the slice will be open-ended. A hyperbola.

My path to and from the moon is constructed, mathematically speaking, of these various slices. Circles and sections of circles, and ellipses, and hyperbolas. You start out with an orbit that's circular, or perhaps slightly elliptical. Then second cosmic velocity puts you on a hyperbola, an open-ended path that will never come back to Earth. Except it passes close enough to the moon that the moon slings you around, again on another hyperbola. And this, in turn, must intersect the earth's path—all while the earth is moving around the sun and the moon is moving around the earth.

If it intersects Earth's path at a proper angle, then, fine, you will reenter. But if it doesn't, you will be in trouble. Beyond the aforementioned possibilities (a ballistic reentry, or skipping at a wrong angle), you might be in an extremely elliptical orbit. And it will only decay if the small end of the ellipse passes through the upper atmosphere. If not, you might be up there for months or years. Decades, even. Or you may end up on yet another hyperbolic path. Open-ended. Going God knows where.

My path should have been a free-return trajectory as soon as we left Earth orbit, before we discarded the Block-D stage. But it wasn't. They were wrong in measuring my telemetry. And the S5.53 can't get me back on course. But we can fix it with the thrusters. I am confident. We will nudge the end of the hyperbola back into place.

• • •

In the morning I eat, floating free, staring out at the heavens. It is still strange to stargaze at breakfast. Since we are not in shadow, I cannot see many stars, but there are a few. How many of them have planets, little earths of their own? How many of those planets have sent voyagers into the cosmos? For all I have seen and done and learned, I will never know the answer.

As for the planets I do know about, I can see Mars and Jupiter, but Venus is lost in the sun's glare. We may visit these in my lifetime, but I'm less optimistic now that Sergei

Pavlovich is gone. As for whether or not we'll find life there, who can say?

I feel melancholy, knowing I'll be an observer at best for all of that; one way or another, I've reached my limits, and the best I can hope for is to come humbly home.

I did not sleep terribly well. I am eager to get back to Valya and the children, to eat a real meal, to sleep in my own bed. I believe it will happen, but only if we work hard.

Komarov is on the console again. We chat briefly. I miss Blondie, but old man Komarov is a good man, too. I know he will do all he can.

I type in the commands. We are going to do a 10-second thruster burn and allow the ballistics center to compute our revised trajectory. We will then have to do additional burns until we're back on track.

When the timer counts down, I press the button and there is a gentle reassuring push from the thrusters.

"Very good, Yura," Komarov says.

We cut the thrusters at the appointed time.

After some minutes, the ballistics center has done their work. They have run the numbers through their giant computers and determined that I need an additional 30 meters per second of delta-v to get back on target for the reentry corridor. We will be tight on the propellant, but we should be able to do that. The second correction is scheduled for after lunch.

My mealtime passes peacefully. It occurs to me that I will miss these quiet times, this solitude. If past experience is any guide, I will not have any time to myself for some while. More press conferences and tours and foreign trips to tropical lands: perhaps they will at least be more forgiving in their scheduling this time.

After everything is cleaned up, I strap myself back in. The ballistics center wants to do another solar alignment before the next burn. I page through the binder and punch in the commands. As usual, the craft swings about.

But this time it keeps moving.

The sun slices lazily past the porthole, and then the moon, receding but still large, and then the distant Earth, and then I see the sun coming around again.

In my heart there is a pang. I take a deep breath. "Solar alignment has failed. Solar alignment has failed," I transmit. I look at the instrument panel briefly, but it only confirms what I already know. "We are tumbling at a rate of approximately 30 degrees per second."

The delayed response: "Cedar, we understand," Komarov says. "30 degrees per second."

And now the sun and moon and earth are moving faster. "Dawn-2, my rate of yaw is increasing. We might have a stuck thruster. Switching to manual controls."

"Understood, Cedar."

I key in the commands and manipulate the thrusters. It is a yawing motion; the spacecraft is spinning like a skidding car.

I apply thrusters in the direction opposite the rotation and it slows. I bring the earth into view. But when I take my hands off the controls, I see it moving again.

"Dawn-2, the thruster is still stuck."

Again I start working the controls. By applying full opposite thruster, I can arrest the motion, but I cannot move back in the opposite direction. This tells me the thruster is still stuck and still firing, and when we are stopped, it is only because both yaw thrusters are firing in the opposite direction, counteracting one another. Which also means we're wasting fuel.

"Cedar, understand you are still rotating about the y-axis."

I am in a bind. This needs to be stopped. And I cannot keep doing what I have been doing, because it isn't working.

Finally I move my hand controller *with* the direction of rotation and then back. And somehow this works, and everything stabilizes. "Dawn-2, we have stopped rotating."

Of course, we are still back where we were before we attempted the solar alignment: we still need to do an alignment before we can fire the thrusters, and we still need to fire the thrusters to get home.

I am waiting for an answer. I try again: "Dawn-2, this is Cedar. Rotation is stopped. How do you wish to proceed?"

"Cedar, we will try the solar alignment once more using the backup thrusters."

Again I key in the commands. Again the spacecraft keeps rotating. This time I grab for the controllers quickly to arrest the motion.

"Solar alignment has failed. Solar alignment has failed." I take a few deep breaths.

There is a period of deliberation down below. Bruised egos battling intellectually in the measured way we have described to keep human passions to a minimum. A competition of sorts, but with strict rules. Almost like a fencing match. All arguments and voices carefully kept in check. And I know that at the end, when all the points are tallied up and graded, they are going to give me their best advice.

At last, I get it: "Yura, we believe it is a short in the controllers. We are going to deactivate the yaw thrusters. We will read up the coordinates and see if you can align manually using the other thrusters. Then we will isolate and fire the pitch thrusters only in translation mode. This should help us avoid further rotation."

"Understood, Dawn-2."

"Your peroxide levels are low. We do not want to waste fuel on further alignments. We are going to have you fire the thrusters until exhaustion. We believe this will still get you in the upper limit of the reentry corridor."

Everything is, as the Americans say, up in the air. Or beyond that, even. Komarov and the control center are projecting a certain optimism, but they're also refusing to make firm predictions. And I understand. We are beyond the outer limits of what anyone thought possible, so there is no use asking for certainty or even probability.

They read up the new procedure and I copy everything down in my logbook. I wonder in passing: are the Americans and the British still listening? Surely this will be of interest to them. Will they tell the world about my troubles before we do?

"It's a good thing this is all just a communications exercise," I joke.

A delay. Then: "Repeat your last, Yura." Komarov is slow in both ways today.

"Dawn-2, I said it's a good thing this is all a communications exercise, and not a real mission. Otherwise I would really be in trouble."

"Indeed, Yura." I am still not sure he gets it.

Once the yaw thrusters have been deactivated I rotate the craft to get the sun in the alignment telescope crosshairs. Then I translate along the rotational coordinates they have provided, keeping a careful eye on my instruments.

"Good luck, Yura," Komarov says.

"Go to hell, old man."

I fire the thrusters. Feel the spacecraft's gentle push. I watch the counters turn. Far too soon, they stop.

•••

I have talked about disasters, but I've only hinted at my own.

If I'm speaking more truthfully about my past, I should at least talk about my time in the whirlwind, the strangeness and dislocation I felt when everything was out of my control.

Flashbulbs, motorcades, flashbulbs, microphones. There were moments, like the ones I've described in Moscow and Manchester and London, where I feel like I handled everything very well indeed. And again, on the whole, I'm proud of my conduct.

But there were also moments where I felt like I was being blown about by forces far greater than me, like in those first few parachute jumps when you step out into the slipstream and you feel your body violently jerked about, pulled and pushed and buffeted, a victim of pure physics.

My mind sometimes felt like that. Particularly at the receptions.

It was strange walking through the room at the receptions. It was as if there was some electromagnetic force field around me; people oriented themselves like filings on paper when you pass a magnet underneath. I would move through the room and the whole human content of the room would move around me. Here and there I was uncomfortable; I'd want to go find some privacy and relax. While they were content to just be in my presence, smiling.

And yet there was still that barrier—the paper between the magnet and the filings. Or perhaps it was a glass wall. For I could see them, and there was still the effect of the magnet passing through the barrier, but I felt separate, strangely isolated in those crowded rooms.

(Also there was this—a real man discovers his worth in overcoming difficulties. And certainly I had done so in flying school, and as a pilot. But in the mission itself? I had been nothing but a passenger. Even during the reentry: if, hypothetically speaking, I had panicked, it all would have gone the same way. I had done nothing beyond the capabilities of any pilot in our air force, but I was being treated like something else entirely.)

So what else was there to do but drink? I had been keeping myself well-behaved up to that time—for fear of turning out like my father, it must be said—but now, after accomplishing something no one else had ever done, what reason did I have not to? So many of the leaders did, after all. Plus, they were toasting my health at every turn. It would have been rude to refuse.

So I drank, at every function. And it made me feel like the glass wall was gone for a moment—like I had a true connection with the people lining up to see me. But—I suppose I can admit to this now—when the glass wall fell, it made the whirlwind worse. For I was fully exposed.

(Am I mixing metaphors here? Providing too many images? It must be done. Words and images are less exact than equations, less precise in modeling our behavior.)

Still, I'm not comfortable talking about it. I have spoken in a general sense; you can perhaps imagine the specifics.

The only man I know who is truly comfortable in such situations is Vladimir Vysotsky. Vysotsky is of course an artist, a singer and actor. As such, he must put his flaws on display, which has in turn led to considerable popularity. (Surely you already know all this!) He has not found official favor, but he has certainly been to many unofficial parties of officials, at the dachas of the mighty out in the birch forests around Moscow, and even at our communal apartments in Star City. In fact, we've had him over a few times, most recently a few months back.

That party got off to a rather raucous start—cosmonauts and pilots tend to be punctual, even in our partying! And he of course was late, but he showed up, guitar in hand, perhaps a bit drunk already.

"Ninety minutes, comrade!" I exclaimed as Valya opened the door. "These delays are not acceptable in our line of work!"

"He has to get soaked!" Blondie yelled from behind me. (We'd instituted a tradition in the cosmonaut corps of dunking late guests in the bathtub, which perhaps contributed to everyone's promptness.)

"He doesn't have to get soaked," I said. "Come in, comrade, come in."

"I am not late," he said in his famous gravelly voice. "I have been partying for the appropriate length of time, just not here. Nor am I a comrade. I am fast on my way to becoming an official scoundrel, regardless of who is listening to me in private. Which is perhaps the way I want it."

"Well, we've been listening," my wife exclaimed. "You'll have to play us a song."

"No hello, even?" he asked with a grin, then gave her the customary kisses on the cheeks. "Aren't you glad to see me?"

"Of course we're glad. Now play us a song!"

"Yes, play us a song," I echoed.

Here he looked suddenly reluctant. "Sure, if you fly around the moon!"

I'm sure I gave him a look.

He explained: "This is a party. Nobody is asking you to do your work!"

"But you're an entertainer," Valya said.

"So I must work while you are having fun." Now he sounded deadly earnest, and I wondered if we'd overstepped our bounds. To Blondie he raised his voice: "Do you see why I took my time getting here?"

"But...you brought your guitar..." Valya said, confused.

He looked down at the guitar case at the end of his hand as if this was the first time he'd seen it. "The guitar came of its own accord. It hitched a ride on my hand. I am so used to seeing it there that I paid it no heed until now."

Valya looked truly baffled. I suppressed a chuckle.

At last, Vysotsky smiled. "But since it is there, I suppose I should play something. As long as you get me a drink first."

Valya poured him a cognac, and he made the rounds of the room: Blondie and his wife, old man Komarov and his, Popovich, Tereshkova, Nikolayev, and assorted other cosmonauts and engineers in various stages of inebriation. And there was some chaos and confusion, the normal disorientation of a disruption to the party, and there was discussion of where he should play, and he disappeared into the bathroom for what seemed like a long while, but at last he emerged and Valya had placed a chair in the center of the room, and he sat down to play. And the room went quiet; everyone's conversations ended as they turned to face him.

And he sang a new song, one I'd never heard, but it sounded instantly familiar, perfect and true, as if it had somehow always existed:

> *I am an exotic man, to put it mildly,*
> *My tastes and my demands are rather strange,*
> *I can, for instance, nibble glasses madly,*
> *And read the works of Schiller for a change.*
>
> *I have two selves in me, two poles of planet,*
> *Two absolutely different men, two foes,*
> *When one is eager to attend a ballet*
> *The other straight off to the races goes.*
>
> *I don't take liberties, when I turn out*

To be myself, going the whole hog,
My other self will frequently break out
Appearing as a rascal and a rogue.

And I oppress the scoundrel's intrusion,
My life! I've never known such distress.
Perchance (I am so scared of confusion),
I'm not that other self whom I oppress.

When in my soul I open up the facets
In spots where sincerity should be
I pay the waitresses, on trust, in assets,
And women give me all their love for free.

But suddenly all my ideals go to grass, as
I'm impatient, angry, rude and such a bore!
I sit like mad, devouring the glasses,
And throwing Schiller down upon the floor.

The hearing is on. I stand and speak austerely,
Appealing to the jury, showing tact:
"It wasn't me who'd smashed the window, really,
It was my other wicked self, in fact.

Do not be strict to me. You'd better
Give me a chance, but not a prison term.
I'll visit court-rooms just as a spectator,
And drop in on the judges as a chum.

I won't smash windows any more, distinctly,
Nor fight in public—write it in your scroll!
I'll bring the halves of my split, sickly,
Disintegrated soul into a single whole.

I'll root it out, bury it and quench it;
I want to clear and reveal my soul.

My other self is alien to my nature,
No, it is not my other self, at all.

He looked straight at me as he sang the last two verses. (Surely this is the power in such a work: you hear it and assume it is about you!) And no one else was singing along: the room was a complete standstill, and I wondered if they thought the same. And I touched the scar on my eyebrow, the one from Foros, the public proof of my secret shame.

But Vysotsky said nothing. And it occurred to me that nobody had sung along because they didn't know the words, either, for it was a new song.

Then came old familiar songs that got everyone singing and clapping. I had almost forgotten the first one when at last he said, "I'm thirsty. Has the state released me from my performing duties?" And I smiled and gave him a hug, and we went over to the kitchen to fix more drinks. And I told him, "You're too hard on the state, my friend," and he said, "I've just made a different choice than you." And I did not know what he meant, but later in the party I asked him, and he said: "Honest, intelligent, loyal to the state. God loves trinity, but we are a godless state, so we cannot have all three. Which two do you choose?" And I said, "You're talking like a degenerate," and he said, "At least I know that's what I am!"

I was furious—why was he making such a scene? But Blondie came up and clapped him on the back and then everything changed, all was forgotten, and it all started blurring together at last in the usual happy drunken way, and it occurred to me that perhaps he was trying to be brave, by his own absurd standards.

In the harsh Sunday morning light, when Valya and I were cleaning up, I came across the lyrics to the song. They were sitting there in the middle of the dining room table where we could hardly miss them; they were scribbled in a drunken scrawl, which (given his lifestyle) did not necessarily mean that he'd written them down last night, but I couldn't help thinking he had, that he'd wanted me to have them.

I threw them away. But not before I'd memorized them.

•••

Lunch passes in melancholy silence.

The ballistics center has been running more calculations. They're projecting that we are close to the upper end of the reentry corridor, but they are not willing to define "close." The controllers and I know there is very little we can do to adjust our trajectory now, except to attempt to fire the reentry thrusters once we cast off the instrument-aggregate compartment. But the reentry thrusters are only meant for rotation, rather than translation—usually when one fires, the one on the opposite side of the craft fires in the opposite direction—so they have to figure out if we can even use them this way. Also, the compartment's meant to be cast off right before reentry; it holds the solar panels and most of the oxygen tanks, so once it's gone we will have a very limited amount of power and oxygen left—enough for reentry, plus reserves. Not enough to last very long if I'm stranded in orbit.

In the meantime we get to work on more immediate issues. We still need to be rotating about the solar axis so as to even out the heating and cooling on various sides of the craft. We had to stop the rotation to attempt our course corrections. But now that the instrument-aggregate thrusters are exhausted, we don't have a good way to start it back up.

What's worse, the voltmeters indicate that the current's erratic now: the panels are angled in relation to the sun, and they cannot draw full power that way. This is what forces us to act. We're still far enough from Earth that we can't get back there on the buffer batteries. We have to restart the rotation before the ship starts dying.

"Dawn-2, this is Cedar. The current from the panels is low. Do you have a plan to restart rotation?"

I wait. The transmission delays are getting shorter.

"Cedar, Dawn-2." Komarov, again. "We'll have to do it with the reentry thrusters."

"Understood." We have no other choice: technical specifications and the simple laws of physics have barricaded us into a narrow path.

"This will be a tricky burn, Yuri. Since it's only the reentry thrusters, we'll need to fire the pitch thrusters as well to cancel out the pitch moment."

The reentry thrusters are only on the descent module. Because they're only meant to be fired when the instrument-aggregate compartment's been cast off, they're lined up with the descent module's center of mass, so as to impart rotation along only one axis. But with the instrument-aggregate compartment attached, the roll thruster will cause the combined spacecraft to rotate along more than one axis. There will be a pitching motion as well, which they need to cancel with the opposite pitch thruster.

"Do you have instructions?"

An awkward pause: "We would prefer to do it under ground control, Yura."

"Very well." I press the buttons to allow them to take over, and I settle back. I know when it's time to do what I'm told. "Ground control enabled."

Since these thrusters are directly attached to my module, I can feel the vibrations more intensely as they fire. I watch the instruments. Soon the voltmeters show more current coming from the solar panels—the normal rise and fall as the panels go broadwise, then edgewise, then broadwise.

"Cedar, this is Dawn-2. Confirm you are rotating again."

"Dawn-2, there is a little wobble, but it's as good as it can be. Thank you much."

"Thank you, Yura."

Soon it is the dinner period. I eat halfheartedly.

I close the working porthole cover and place the temporary paper shield over the other. I can shut out the sun but cannot turn off my mind.

The sheer number of technical issues on this mission seems to defy all logic and probability. The problems with the stellar alignment telescope, and the unnecessary waste of propellant because of it. The S5.53 failing. The problem with the stuck thruster that caused us to consume most of the rest of the propellant.

When you are awake, your thoughts are ordered and rational, logical and smooth like glass. But in the night the clear glass shatters and everything is sharp and strange and chaotic.

●●●

I find my mind wandering back to Komarov, to the launch that had been scheduled for late April.

There had been problems developing the Union. Everyone knows it is the craft of the future—even my moon ship is derived from it—but it was not quite ready. The unmanned test craft had failed.

It seemed they were planning on launching anyway. But there was a technical report detailing ongoing issues with the craft that needed to be resolved. Was I influenced by what Vysotsky had said about the state? Was it some other factor, some defiance that had been growing in me? I do not know. But I saw to it that the right people saw this report. Never mind how—I made sure that the State Commission didn't rubber-stamp the approval for Komarov's mission. Instead they decided on an additional test flight—during which the parachutes failed, necessitating a redesign of the parachute compartments.

Given these disruptions, and their desire to top Gemini, the circumlunar flight became more and more appealing. But I cannot help thinking that I made some enemies during all of this.

In my rational mind, I know these thoughts don't make sense. People are not quite that evil in real life, only in the movies. Still there is that nagging thought: would anyone be happy if I don't come back?

•••

Usually I look at the hammer and sickle and see it as it's supposed to be: a symbol of the revolution. Workers and peasants united. And yet the two can be understood differently.

You probably haven't heard of Nelyubov. I won't go into details, but suffice it to say he was an alcoholic, and he disgraced himself. And after his night of disaster, and before they sent him off, he described the hammer and sickle to me in this negative sense. He said: The state has to cut you down to size, and it has to hammer you into line.

As deputy chief of cosmonaut training, I had to do my share of hammering. But usually the discipline fell to Kamanin. And while Nelyubov got the worst of it, none of us has entirely avoided our time beneath the hammer.

During one of my goodwill trips to Paris, back in 1965 or so, I'd been given a beautiful sports car, a red Matra. It was an exquisite ride, a jet on wheels, and I enjoyed it immensely.

On one boring day back at the training center, Blondie and I started talking about it over lunch. He wanted to see what it could do, so I took him for a ride. When the guard opened the gate, we tore off, ripping down the back roads, raising rooster tails of dust. As usual for us, we got into a heated discussion; we were headed down the road at a good 160 kilometers an hour, and I took my hands from the wheel to make an emphatic point. And his eyes—oh, the look in his eyes! It was a couple seconds before he realized I was steering with my knees. I pointed—got you!—and put my hands back on the wheel.

It was a while before I could talk, I was laughing so hard. When we finally stopped at the next crossroads, I told him: "You should see your face! You went white!"

He shook his head, chuckling now at last. "And you were red, you were laughing so hard."

"Better red than dead," I said: a little slogan, something I had heard a while before.

We were still laughing on the way back through the gate at Star City. The guard saluted but did not make eye contact with me. When we made it back to the office, I found out why.

"Yuri, your car is…attracting attention," Kamanin said.

"Attention from whom. The guards?"

"I ordered them to keep an eye out. I got a phone call last week about it from Suslov. From Suslov!" (He was agitated— Suslov was and is, of course, a Politburo member; this was not long after Khruschev's fall, and everyone knew Suslov had Brezhnev's ear.) "There were photographs of you in the Western papers."

"He shouldn't have been reading them," I pointed out.

Kamanin glared.

"It's the only way I get to fly these days," I added.

"Yuri, you know how these things appear. Word gets around. We all know we're in a…privileged place. But only by virtue of the great things we're doing. So we don't want to be flashy about it."

"Suslov…" I seethed. "They're bureaucrats. We, you and I, have risked our lives for the state."

"For the state, or for yourself?" he asked. "Look, Yuri, you're a good party member, by and large. You need to be less flashy. The car's…bright. Very noticeable."

"We're living simply here. They offered to build us dachas. Brezhnev himself offered dachas for the whole cosmonaut corps. I turned him down so we could live communally, in apartments."

"A dacha is quiet and out of the way, at least. This…"

"Are you ordering me to get rid of it? It might be bad for morale…if we don't get to do anything extra, what are we risking our lives for?"

"You don't have to get rid of it. Just…paint it, perhaps."

"So my car's too red. It's too red, so it isn't red enough. And if it was less red, then it would be more red."

"If it was less red, you would look more red," Kamanin pointed out.

"Very well, I'll have it painted black. I'm sorry if I put you in a bad spot."

"I knew you'd understand," Kamanin said, at last.

It only occurred to me afterwards that the state really didn't know what to do with me. Khrushchev had fallen, and I was associated with Khrushchev, but they could not get rid of all of yesterday's heroes. I'd been put on a lot of posters. The imagery of my flight had become central to the state's sense of self: the imagery of progress, of undeniable accomplishment.

Surely you have seen these images! (I, myself, did not see them until later.) The tremendous concrete basin, like something from Stalin's wet dreams. The steel support arms falling away and the R-7 rising, standing steady on a tower of fire. The massive concrete pit now filling with flame. The shot down at the rocket's shadow moving away from the launch pad. A dark dart, a shadow ship sailing smoothly across the steppe, with a heatwave wake trailing behind. Then from orbit: a blurry television image. My black-and-white eyes. Smile hidden by the spacesuit's neck ring.

And of course, the reception in Moscow. My flapping shoelace as I walked across the tarmac to report to Khrushchev. Then, the motorcade. Me riding up front with Khrushchev, and Korolev a few cars behind us, unheralded and anonymous. The solid red mass of Lenin's tomb. Then: standing up there. Smiling and waving. Innocent. Everyone has seen these things, and so have I. But to them they are real, and to me they are just shadows of what I saw.

As I said before, there were posters in the crowd, gigantic posters of Lenin, and posters of me, just as large.

Image is, of course, important, but only to a point. When you look at a poster, do you stop and think what it conceals? For surely a poster's a way of saying: "Look at this! Don't look at whatever's behind this, look at this!" Does it matter what's behind it? Perhaps. If the poster's attached to a cement wall, it's incidental; you can replace it as needed. But if the backing is rotting, worm-eaten wood, the poster may be the only thing holding it together. At some point, that's a lot to ask of a poster.

Some were saying I didn't deserve the attention, that I, after all, hadn't done anything to compare with the heroes of the Great Patriotic War. (Surely this is one of the defining facts of 20th century life—if you were an adult in the second half of the century, you must hear endlessly from those who lived through the first half about how good you have it, how you don't know what it's like to endure hardship. As if my family didn't endure the German occupation! As if I didn't see my own brother hung to within an inch of his life!)

These were all just whispers. But I knew I would be a fool if I ignored them. Especially after that talk with Kamanin. I sent the car to the garage to be painted, and soon it was October, and it seemed wise to leave it inside all winter, until the various storms blow over.

Soon afterwards, in early 1966, there was a retrospective on state television on the fifth anniversary of my flight, April 12th, which is now of course called Cosmonautics Day. Valya insisted I watch it at home with the girls, and I couldn't help but notice everything had been edited, shortened, changed. Virtually every shot of Khrushchev had been taken out; it was as if I'd gone into space of my own accord, a spontaneous ascension into the heavens, the glorification of one man as representative of the people. No mention of Khrushchev at all.

He is not dead, of course. Such things happened under Stalin; people were erased from the official photographs as they fell out of favor, and it always meant they were dead. (Such things have even happened recently! Bondarenko, for instance, was removed from some photographs after his death, which has helped feed the absurd rumors about lost cosmonauts. I don't know if I'll have a chance to tell you about Bondarenko. Suffice it to say it was a tragic story, an absurd little catastrophe that did not bring credit to anyone involved.) Khrushchev has been edited out, but he is simply on house arrest. So the state is not so cruel any more. But clearly even Khrushchev is dispensable.

And despite all the attention I've gotten, I know that everyone is, in the end, dispensable. Even me. Even you. If you drop dead tomorrow, those around you may mourn, but they will get along without you.

But I made up my mind, after that talk with Kamanin, that I wouldn't give them reason to carry on without me. As much as I hate to say it, it was an incentive: to cut back on the drinking, to get my head down and work, to find a way back up here.

•••

In the night, time passes strangely.

With the interior lights off and the shades in place, I can only see by the soft glow of the panel, the pushbuttons and the gauges and the voltmeter.

Before East-1, one of the automated test flights had oriented itself improperly before it fired its retrorockets. It was supposed to turn itself so the engine was facing in the direction of the orbital sunrise, just as my flight would do some months later. But it did the opposite, and instead of causing the orbit to decay, the retrorocket pushed it into a higher orbit. It did not fall back to earth until 1965.

If I miss the atmosphere, I will end up in an elliptical orbit. We may exhaust the reentry thrusters to try and lower the low point of the orbit. There is no clear place where the atmosphere ends and space begins, but if we bring the low point low enough, atmospheric drag will eventually bring me down.

I wonder, briefly, how long my ordeal will last. Then I remind myself: it is pointless to speculate on such matters.

I find myself thinking of Maresyev flying over a sea of trees, the undulating green of a vast forest. Then shot down, stranded in those woods, hobbling on shattered feet for 18 days until he reached Soviet lines. (And afterwards, of course, learning to dance on wooden feet so he could convince the doctors he was fit enough to fly.)

I think, too, of the old man in Hemingway's book, far out in the blue sea, battling the giant fish, hands cut and bleeding, and no one there to help him. I read it again recently, and now various phrases are floating through my mind. One about how the old man took his suffering as it came. And the old man's assessment of the fish: his fight has no panic in it. And another about the old man, when he was in the midst of his ordeal: he tried not to think, but only to endure.

•••

On January 12, 1966, Blondie and I went to Sergei Pavlovich's house to celebrate his fifty-ninth birthday.

We came bearing a bronze statue, a heavy sculpture of a man ascending towards the heavens. Every member of the cosmonaut corps had signed it, and there was a plaque at its base that said: *TO THE STARS*.

It was quite a task wrestling that statue out of my car and up to his apartment—it weighed 50 kilograms! The walks were icy, and we were slipping and sliding and swearing; Blondie even tore a button from his overcoat.

But at last, upstairs, we presented it to him, and there were tears in his eyes, and we knew our efforts had been worthwhile. Few men truly get to know that their life's work has made a difference; we wanted to make sure he knew that he was the one truly indispensable man in all of this, in all of our lives and careers and explorations.

His apartment filled up—engineers, cosmonauts, family, servants. I remember meat and cabbage pies, and cognac. We drank many toasts, and we ate so much that it did not matter how much we drank.

And when at last everyone had gone, all the servants had retired and Korolev's wife had gone to bed, and we were finally going to leave, Korolev motioned for us to stay.

And he started to talk. He spoke with the looseness and freedom that, in our country, only comes late at night among close friends when one is drunk.

"You men have been chosen by the state to receive tremendous things." His voice was strangely serious. "All the honors and accolades the country can offer. But the state only gives what it has the power to take away."

Blondie and I glanced over at one another. Neither of us said anything.

"I'm sure you see me as a good Soviet man. A perfect member of the state. Humble and anonymous, content only to build the rockets and let the state have the glory. I suppose that's how I want to be seen these days."

He motioned for a cigarette. He did not normally smoke. I provided him with one and lit it, and he kept on: "In 1938, the NKVD came in the night to get me. They were rounding up a lot of people in those days, but it was the sort of thing we only talked about in whispers. They came for me in the night and did not even give me a chance to bid my family goodbye.

"Before I knew it, I was in some dank holding cell in some subterranean jail. They saw to it that I did not sleep. Periodically they took me in for questioning. I lost all track of time. They tortured me. At one point, they smashed a pitcher of water against my head and broke my jaw. And I did not even know why I had been arrested until they brought me in for my so-called 'trial.'

"When it was time for this 'trial,' I felt a little better, for I knew the men running it. There was a troika of judges, led by a party official named Voroshikov, whom I'd met socially on several occasions. But that day there was a deadness in his eyes; it was as if he'd never met me. He handed me a paper alleging that I had funneled funds from an agricultural institute to set up a new design bureau for rocketry. He asked me if it was true, and I said, 'No.' Then one of the other judges said, 'All these bastards say they're innocent. Give him ten years.'

"From there I was shipped to Kolyma, to the gold mines. A long journey by train, east across the country in boxcars, shitting and pissing in pots. Then by boat across the sea of Okhotsk, north to this godforsaken spot of far Siberia. It was awful work, exhausting work. Clearing trees and mining. Watching one's fellow prisoners get thinner and thinner and thinner, and realizing it was happening to you, too, that the skin was drawing tighter over your bones, and the shape of your skeleton was becoming evident.

"I was there for a year. And I would have died, had I spent another year there. The fact that I lived is somewhat providential. I am not a religious man, but there were several unlikely factors which saved my life.

"First, it became apparent to those in power that they should not be sending talented people to slave away doing manual labor in gold mines when they could instead make us slave away doing engineering work for the aircraft industry. So I was recalled to Moscow.

"Of course, the camps were a great distance from the port—far off in the back country. So I had to hitch a ride by truck back to Magadan. The driver only took me when I gave him my boots in exchange for his worn-out shoes. We got back to

Magadan in the afternoon, and it turned out that the last ship of the season had sailed that morning. I later found out that that ship had sunk with all hands. Again, fate had spared me. Or God. Whatever you prefer."

Blondie and I sat there, rapt. Time and tiredness melted away. All that remained was the story.

Korolev continued: "Of course, I was on my own for food and shelter. The truck driver had gone, and I certainly wasn't about to go back to the mines. I stumbled about on the outskirts of town; I was hungry and out of my mind and nearing collapse. And I found a loaf of bread by the side of the road. A fresh, pure, new loaf of bread. I wolfed it down and gained strength to go on and eventually snuck in to another camp, into a worker's barracks. And I told them about the bread, and they laughed. They thought it was impossible. In that part of the country, bread was more precious than gold. Nobody would have just dropped a loaf by the side of the road.

"In the springtime I finally caught a ship to Vladivostok. Conditions at the worker's barracks were better than the mines, but it still had been a miserable winter. I was famished, gaunt and skeletal, and my teeth were falling out from scurvy. The authorities put me on a train back to Moscow, but I was taken off halfway because it was feared I might die. And it just so happened that there was a healer in that town, a wild man who lived in a cave on a hillside. Some old lady summoned him, and he rubbed herbs on my gums and fed me broth, and in a week I had my strength back.

"I spent the rest of the war in a compound near Moscow, working on projects for the state and for various bureaus. We were still prisoners, but at least we were well-fed, and working with our minds, rather than our bodies. And the war ended, and they needed people with knowledge of rocketry to go to Germany and figure out what the Germans had done with the A-4. And I went, and I made myself useful. So the next thing I know, I was made a colonel. My past was forgiven.

"Because of my accomplishments in that field, I became valuable to the state. I was not officially rehabilitated until 1957, but I was at least valuable. I could not help but sense that I had been saved by Divine Providence, though, saved for a purpose, saved to help accomplish this grand goal, of sending man into the heavens. All that Tsiolkovsky dreamed about and wrote about and researched, I was to bring to fruition.

"But of course, the state kept me anonymous. The Chief Designer. And they did not let any of us publish under our own names, nor did they praise us publicly. I'm told that the Nobel Prize committee even asked Khrushchev for my name; they wanted to give me the Nobel Prize for physics. And Nikita Sergeyevich told them that it was an accomplishment of the whole people. They have circulated their reasons for all of this, all those paranoid Stalinist fantasies about foreign agents and saboteurs waiting to assassinate us should our names be publicly known. But other names have been known. Kurchatov was the father of the atomic bomb, and everyone knew who he was before he died. So I cannot help but think that, in my case, there is another reason: the state cannot afford to admit to mistakes. If there is officially no God, then the state must appear to be infallible. Otherwise people will look elsewhere for their peace of mind."

Blondie and I looked at one another. Neither of us had heard any of this. What was I feeling? Anger? Frustration? Sadness? Perhaps many things at once. But one also must grow numb.

There were many things we could have said, but we became aware of our tiredness, of the lateness of the hour. We left in a somber mood.

Two days later, Sergei Pavlovich was dead.

He'd been scheduled for surgery to remove a polyp in his colon. The minister of health himself was performing the surgery. But Korolev started to bleed profusely. They'd tried to intubate him, but since his jaw had been broken all those years ago, the surgeons could not get the tube down into his airway.

After his death, his identity was revealed at last. *Truth* made his death front-page news, and he was no longer merely the Chief Designer. He was cremated and interred with full honors in the Kremlin wall. A televised funeral with Mozart's *Requiem* playing, and all the ceremony the state could muster.

Brezhnev spoke; he gave a brief mention of Korolev's ordeal, which surprised me, for I'd expected none. And I gave the eulogy; I scarcely remember what I said, but as I surveyed the expectant faces in Red Square, I was glad at last that Sergei Pavlovich was finally getting the praise and recognition that he deserved; he deserved it, indeed, far more than I did.

When all that was over, several of us gathered at the apartment of Boris Chertok, one of Korolev's chief deputies, to eat chocolate and drink cognac and reminisce. All of us were still stunned by the turn of events; Komarov in particular was insistent that there be an investigation into Korolev's death.

Do I believe the state killed him? No, of course not. (Unless, of course, one considers all the damage done to his health by his time in the camps, in which case they did indeed kill him, but in a rather delayed manner, like cigarettes do.) I suppose what I mean is this: Korolev was hardly the picture of health when he went in for that fatal surgery; he'd had a heart attack in 1960 for instance, and the doctors had warned him to lessen his workload, but he hadn't listened. And indeed, the official report on his death said the operation had uncovered a fist-sized cancer in his lower abdomen, one that would have killed him in a few months even if he'd never gone in for surgery.

Still, I couldn't help but wonder if they'd botched the operation, and then lied about the tumor to deflect attention from themselves. The state cannot afford to admit to mistakes.

And it occurs to me now that, as far as the state is concerned, a dead hero might be more useful than a live one: you can put whatever words you want into the mouth of a dead hero. You can fill his life with your own meanings.

•••

Morning.

What I thought would be my last full day up here. (Now all I can say is: it's the last day of the trip back.)

I uncover the portholes and sunlight stabs my eyes. The craft is still rotating. Because of the angle of the windows relative to our flight path, I cannot see much of the earth—just a sliver when my head is very near the hull of the ship, and only when the wobble in the rotation is just right. But I know it is getting bigger. We are moving faster.

After taking care of various bodily functions, I decide to call down to the control center. Unlike Hemingway's old man, I am not alone, no matter if I feel otherwise.

"Dawn-2, this is Cedar. Dawn-2, this is Cedar."

No response.

"Dawn-2, this is Cedar. Dawn-2, this is Cedar."

Again, nothing.

"Dawn-2, this is Cedar, please come in."

Then: Blondie! "Yura, it is good to hear you!"

"You're back, Blondie!"

"They ordered me to get some rest, Yura. I was too tired to argue." (A crackle.) "...stole my alarm clock. I slept for twelve hours, straight through."

The quickness of the responses reassures me. I am indeed close to home. I grin. "Must be nice, lazy."

"Yura, I tried to stay on the console! I was falling asleep on my feet! They were very concerned!"

I try to keep my voice level. "I'm sure they were, Blondie." At last I chuckle.

"You had me going there, Yura," Blondie says. "You know I will stay here until I drop."

"I know, Blondie."

I do know it. For all my fretting in the night, I do know it.

Again, I don't know who you are, or what prejudices you may have about our system. But for all my occasional disillusionment, I must say this: the normal human bonds of friendship and family are far stronger than anything imposed by the state. I have read the banned books, not just Orwell's *1984*, but also the books it stole from, Zamyatin's *We* and

Koestler's *Darkness at Noon*, and I know it is a staple of these stories to imagine betrayal by a friend or loved one, those closest to you. And such things do happen, here and there, but by and large it is just not the case. (Incidentally, *1984* seems somewhat narcissistic on Orwell's part. To believe that you, as an average citizen, are worth watching by the state, for no reason whatsoever? It defies logic to believe they'd expend that much effort watching you. Me, perhaps, but not you. I'm not trying to be vain here! It's just that the state doesn't care about most people.) I digress. The point is, I know I'm cared for. These friendships, these relationships, all mean something.

"I need to know the schedule for the day. What time do I cast off the instrument-aggregate compartment?"

A delay: "Hold one, Yura."

Mishin comes on: "The State Commission has been discussing your situation, Yura..." (Static.) "...some debate. If you're still not in line with the reentry corridor, it may be best to leave the compartment on. It'll help your orbit decay faster, and if you're up there for..." (Static.) "...it may be necessary to have it so as to not run down the batteries. We can always cast it off once it's clear you're going to reenter."

"Very well." So it's true, then: they don't know how long I will be up here.

Blondie comes back on. "There's someone else who wants to speak to you."

A pause, then a voice: Kamanin. "Yuri, we may need to make an unfortunate announcement."

My throat catches: "What kind of announcement?"

"Yuri, if you don't hit the reentry corridor, we won't know where or when you're coming down. It could take some time for the ballistics center to…" (Static.) "…a partial orbit or an elliptical orbit, and given the inclination, it could be almost anywhere. If it's at sea, it may be that some other country's ships are better positioned to provide assistance. This was obviously not how we wanted to announce this mission to the world, but for your safety, it might be best to make a global announcement, so everyone is prepared."

I think about this. If we manage a ballistic reentry straightaway, it will send me into the Indian Ocean, and we're prepared for that; there are Soviet ships tasked to retrieve me. And the normal reentry profile, the guided skip reentry, will bring me back to a landing on Soviet soil, like every other mission we've had. But this…I imagine the possibilities: Indians, Indonesians, Chinese, Chileans, Brazilians, British, Americans.

At last I respond: "You can hold off on that announcement."

This delay feels long. His response, puzzled: "Hold off?"

"Yes. Don't say anything until it's necessary. When the ballistics center knows when I'm coming down, that's when we should announce it, and only to whomever might be positioned to help."

Blondie comes back on: "You're sure, Yura?"

"I'm sure. There's no need to look foolish."

● ● ●

What else do you wish to know about me? They say actions reveal character, and I've tried to give an honest account of mine. Do you wish to know more, still?

I have told you about catastrophes, but not my own.

Do you want to know about Foros? The truth is I don't remember all that much.

It was September of 1961, just a few months after my flight. Everyone knew I needed a break after the relentless touring, and Titov had just landed, so we were vacationing in the Crimea. We were boating, and we were drinking, and I injured my hand, and they patched me up. Then came more drinking, and I woke up in the hospital.

That's where everything was explained to me, the fall and the surgery, and the fact that I'd have to miss the 22nd Party Congress, which was coming up in a few weeks.

I understand everyone's explanations of my actions, but I still have a hard time believing them. The official story is that I hit my head while trying to grab my daughter and keep her from falling. I can tell you the official story's untrue. I cannot tell you the truth, for I don't know it. It's possible that it happened the way it was explained to me. Still, I can't help thinking that somehow Kamanin had engineered the whole event to discredit me, or at least to have some leverage. Certainly after that I made it a point to be better friends with the agents in my security detail!

There was another night I recall—somewhat—from that December. I believe I was in Ceylon. The whirlwind had stopped, briefly, after Foros, but it had picked up again, and strengthened into a tropical cyclone. Titov was touring too, now, and they'd brought along my wife to keep an eye on me, but it was relentless all the same. Here I was, a world traveler—I, who had never been out of the Soviet Union!— visiting places on a moment's notice after last-minute changes in itinerary, places I had never heard of, places I had to go back and find on maps and globes just to know where I'd been.

So my wife was with me, and our children were back at home with my parents, and we desperately wanted just to go out shopping, to feast our senses on all the local strangeness, the sights and sounds and smells of the bustling markets, the dark-skinned locals and their babbling tongues, the leafy palms and tea trees.

Instead I was making speeches, planting ceremonial trees, meeting with the prime minister. Sitting on the couch for what was ostensibly a chat—as if either of us spoke the other's language!—but was really an excuse for people to take pictures of us together.

It was like I'd been cursed, one of those strange curses in folklore where you asked for something good but weren't specific enough. I'd wanted to see the world; I'd seen it all in 106 minutes. And now I was seeing it again from a lower orbit, one that felt much faster.

I complained to Kamanin briefly, at the end of a grueling day which was to be topped off by a reception at the Soviet embassy. We were alone in the car with Alexei driving and Venyamin riding along and my wife's car following behind. A few precious minutes alone.

"Is something wrong, Yuri?" he asked.

I burst. "We need to slow this down! I'm burned out! I can't enjoy any of it! I went to India, and I met Nehru, but I never saw an elephant!"

"You wouldn't have been picked if you weren't the right man for the job."

"It's too much!"

"It's necessary!" Kamanin exclaimed. "Do you think this is about…seeing elephants? This is necessary!" Briefly he seemed about to lose his composure. But he took a deep breath and continued. "We are…in a competition, Yuri. Our country. Another war. But we have the ability to fight this one in newspapers and on television screens, rather than on the battlefield. No death, no destruction, just…competition. Think about that! Think of all the hardships you're saving us! We've endured two wars this century. The second far worse than the first. The third, if it comes, will be immeasurably worse than the second. But if it doesn't happen…" He stared at me. "We can keep it from happening, Yuri. You can keep it from happening. If they're in awe of our rockets, of our technology…You are the face of that, Yuri! Nobody knows who Sergei Pavlovich is. You are the face of it! Think about that."

I hated to think about it. But he was right. What could I do?

Back at the embassy, there were more photographers, more reporters. We were swept inside on the crest of a wave of people.

I found myself seated at the head table, as usual, throwing back shot after shot with everyone who wanted to drink with me. I'm sure I was a little tipsy by the time the ambassador from the German Democratic Republic came up. His wife eyed me suggestively.

"My wife wanted me to come up and drink a toast with you. But you're already looking a little red!" Slurred but passable Russian. He patted me on the back.

His wife added, in far better Russian: "Back home in the Western Zone, during the August crisis, they were carrying signs saying 'Better red than dead.'"

"We can drink to that, then!" I exclaimed, and my wife gave me an awful look. "Better red than dead!" We drank. And the ambassador's wife looked at me like she'd never been happier.

Soon they were swept away. And the vodka was, in truth, getting to my head, and having its other usual effects, so I headed off to the restroom. And I was walking—one of those drunken walks where it's as if every wall has developed its own gravitational field—and I happened to bump into the ambassador's wife, alone this time. And I sensed that it hadn't been an accident, that she had timed her own trip to the facilities to coincide with mine. And I'm sure I blushed a bit, but truth be told, there was some thrill in knowing she was chasing me. And I was just about at that level of drunkenness where you forget about marriages, rules, commitments—or perhaps you just decide not to care.

Our dialogue went something like this:

She said in my ear: "You look like you need to get away."

I'm sure I turned even redder. "They tend to keep an eye on me at these things nowadays." I nodded towards Alexei.

She smiled. "There's always a way to get away."

"Together?"

"I'll go outside, you go to the bathroom, and you can climb out the window! They don't follow you in there, do they? Come on! It'll be like a secret mission."

I must have murmured some form of assent. In the bathroom, I relieved myself, standing unsteady, doing one-armed push-ups against the wall, and I wobbled back to the sink and eyed myself in the mirror, chuckling at the craziness of it all. But sure enough, I pried open the window and took off my uniform jacket and clambered awkwardly out, and the next thing I knew I was tumbling to the tropical grass with a thud.

I cursed myself. Maybe this was what had happened at Foros, after all. Perhaps it was all happening again. A depressing circularity.

Then I heard laughter. Somehow she was already outside.

"Yuri, are you all right?" The informal *you*—we'd clearly left formality inside.

Against my better judgment I, too, started laughing. "Yes, yes."

"Not as dignified as your last return to earth, I'm sure."

Again I thought of Foros. But of course she was talking about East-1. That's all anyone talks about with me.

"It was another adventure, at least," I smiled. "All right, now where do we go?"

"Why do we need to go anywhere now?" Her face was beautiful in the moonlight: pale, immaculate, pristine. "We're outside, away from the crowd, it's a beautiful night. What else is there?"

She talked as if she knew me. That's the thing about being famous: after all the press conferences and newsreels, after watching you greet so many unfamiliar situations, everyone thinks they know you. And perhaps they do. But you don't know them.

And yet it seemed like I *did* know her. That moment when you see someone and you really make eye contact in a way that energy flows between you—sometimes you have that moment right away.

"Well, let's have a smoke at least," I said. And I rooted about in my pockets, but my cigarettes had been crushed in the fall.

"I've got a few," she said, and pulled a silver cigarette holder from her clutch.

And in my drunken state I said, "Do you want to go anywhere?" and she said I'd already asked that.

I don't know what I wanted, what I expected. You can ascribe all sorts of motives, and in truth, in drunkenness our motives so frequently get distorted and tangled and lost. But my heart was heavy, and even the alcohol hadn't gotten rid of that. And I wanted so much. Maybe I just wanted to explore the city as a normal man, to spend time as a real man, not an icon or a poster or a photo opportunity. To wander empty streets, to walk along the beach and dip my feet in tropical surf. Or to fly above it all, swoop down over the waves...

When I lit my cigarette I took a deep breath and it all fell away. All the weight. We sat and leaned against the embassy wall in the pale moonlight and looked up at the deep blue night and the tropical trees.

"What are those trees?"

She laughed: a most delightful laugh. "You know what a palm tree is, don't you, Yuri?"

"No, I have never heard of palm trees. I am Ivan the Fool. I never left the Soviet Union before this April, and even then I just went once around the world and came back home as quickly as I could, so as to spend as much time as possible in paradise."

Again she laughed. "Really?"

"That is true. I never left the country before this year. But I do know what a palm tree is. No, those other ones…" I pointed.

"They might be cinnamon trees."

Now it was my turn to laugh.

She asked what was funny.

I explained: "When I was a little boy, before the war, my mother made tea cakes, with cinnamon. There were shortages of everything; we were poor country folk in Stalin's Soviet Union. But she had made tea cakes, and she had cinnamon in them, for the first time in a long time. And she gave me one, but I wanted more, so I snuck back to the kitchen and ate all of them. And my father, he was a…cranky drunk, always. And he exploded: 'Cinnamon is scarce, Yuri! But you act as if it's everywhere. You act like it comes from the trees!'"

And she laughed again, a deep and hearty laugh, and I laughed again, and it felt shared and real and true and more genuine than anything.

And the moon was full and gleaming and it occurred to me that there was nothing between it and us but distance. No walls, no barriers, no guards, just distance. What if we could go there?

And perhaps you are wondering what was going to happen next. Would there have been some inappropriate romantic moment with this woman who was not my wife? Well I don't know, either. For there came a whispered angry voice. "Yuri!" Alexei in the shadows, whispering through clenched teeth.

I got up, threw my jacket back on, and realized I was drunker than I thought, and my trousers were torn, and my shirt was untucked. "Just catching some fresh air."

In the moonlight I could tell he was angry and frustrated, the strange strangled feelings of a subordinate and minder who needs to dig his superior out of trouble. "Kamanin is looking for you. And your wife's upset. We need to get you inside now, without anyone seeing."

And we circled the building and there were few enough people out front that it seemed safe, but when we came inside there were faces and voices. "Comrade Gagarin, what were you doing outside?" and "Who is that woman?" and "Look at him, he's drunk!" And there were flashbulbs, flashbulbs, flashbulbs.

And Kamanin glared, as angry as I'd seen him. Still, he did not talk to me but instead turned to the nearest photographer and said he needed the man's film. And I think the man hesitated, but then Alexei reminded him that we were technically on Soviet territory. And the man said we would all be reading about this. But then Kamanin asked if they wanted me to get in trouble when I got back to the Soviet Union. And my wife was watching, and I do believe she was less than pleased, and someone said: "I think he's in trouble already!"

Still, Kamanin and Alexei started taking the cameras from the photographers and pulling out the rolls of film and exposing them. And someone got upset and tried to hold back, but Kamanin whispered something in his ear, and sure enough, he gave up his film to be destroyed.

And then came a loud voice, proclaiming that I was a fake and a phony. It was the German ambassador—and he was more than tipsy himself! He said: The face of the people cannot be drunk!

And I could have hit him, but I did not want to press my luck. Even in my drunken state I knew there were things I could not do. I thought of Nelyubov. I did not want to end up like Nelyubov.

I wobbled, looked around. The ambassador's wife had disappeared.

But the ambassador was there and I clapped him on the back. And perhaps I thought of Kamanin and how it's best to smooth these things over. I think I told him that there had been a great misunderstanding, but drinking was the answer to our misunderstandings. And he said: Then come now, comrade, let's have a drink. And we stumbled off, crunching spent flashbulbs under our shoes and nearly tripping over the rolls of exposed film that were strewn across the wooden floor like party streamers. And I asked why people wanted to take pictures on a night such as this? What was the point of such a night if you couldn't forget what you wanted to forget?

And I wanted to make nice with him and relax and bond with a drink. But I was still curious about where his wife had gone, and I believe I was looking about for her, and he said something to the effect of: What are you looking for, comrade? There is nowhere to go. And I was still mad at him for being such an ass, and I think I spotted his wife across the room, and it occurred to me that I did not even know her name...

And...well, I would love to tell you how the evening ended. But it appears there is no more film in the cameras.

•••

And now we are coming to the end—the end of the planned mission, at least.

I have eaten my lunch and my dinner. Our projections had me landing at a total mission time of 6 days, 18 hours, 24 minutes, give or take. And we are closing in on that.

I am strapped in to my seat, ready to reenter if we catch the atmosphere and slow down enough. The instrument-aggregate compartment is still on, but I must be ready to cast it off at a moment's notice. (The base of the descent module—its all-important heat shield—is covered by the instrument-aggregate compartment, and if we do not discard that once we're in the upper atmosphere, then the craft may tumble and burn up.)

I can see the earth filling the porthole at last. All of you—dear people!—all of you are down there, and I have taken the most magnificent photograph in history, and I desperately want to show it to you, if only I get the chance.

And outside the window I think I see the barest whiff of orange-pink plasma. I think I see it, but I cannot be sure, and perhaps I just think I see it because I'm hoping for it. And I wait for the furnace, I wait for the forge. But nothing happens.

In these moments, I am excited, alive, pulse pounding, full of anticipation. But as it becomes clear that I am not reentering, that feeling falls away, and in its place comes a great weariness.

Before long I am passing into orbital night. I crane my head and catch a sliver of the sunset. I do not know how many more I will see before I fall to earth. I have enough food and oxygen for a few more days, at least. As for what will happen when that runs out—well, I don't want to dwell on that.

It is time to report in.

"Dawn-2, this is Cedar. Dawn-2, this is Cedar."

No response.

"Dawn-2, this is Cedar. Dawn-2, this is Cedar."

Again, nothing.

"Dawn-2, this is…"

"Cedar, this is Dawn-2." Blondie. "You're still up there."

"I am still up here. Temperature and pressure and electrical readings are all normal."

"The State Commission is convening to discuss your situation, Yura. They may make an announcement, depending on the results of the discussion. But they are waiting on calculations from the ballistics center to determine your current trajectory. You're in a highly elliptical orbit. We don't know how soon it will decay."

"Understood, Blondie."

"I talked to Mishin before he left. He mentioned the possibility of turning on your interior camera and having you make a statement."

"Live or taped? Who is the audience?"

"I'm not sure what they're going to allow, Yura. We could do a public statement and a private one. But think about what you might want to say and who you might want to say it to. And we'll see what they permit. Rest assured we won't forget about you, Yura. We won't rest until you're home."

"I know, Blondie."

"How are you feeling?"

"I am tired. I didn't sleep well last night. I may need to take a rest period."

"Very well, Yura. We should have more answers for you on your next pass."

"If I'm awake." I smile.

"We won't wake you unless it's urgent."

"Very well. That is all for now. I do need to sleep, Blondie."

"Very well, Yura."

My body's tired, but my mind is spinning through possibilities. I tell myself it's time to relax. Everything that can be done has been done, for now. There is some peace in that, at least.

For a few seconds my tiredness falls away and I see everything exactly as it is. There is a sharpness and a sense of reality to it all. I scan the instruments. Everything is not as planned, but perhaps it is all as it's supposed to be. And everything—every panel and switch in the old familiar cabin—suddenly looks clear and real and new.

I look up at the perfect circle of the camera lens. Its cold dead gleam. The illumination source is of course turned off. Will they have me make a statement? What is there to say? I can think of a few things, but I will keep them to myself for now.

I turn off the interior lights. I leave my makeshift porthole cover off. I feel confident that the sunlight won't wake me when we pass out of Earth's shadow.

What am I thinking? I'm sure you'd like to know. And I'm sure you'd prefer certain things, depending on your beliefs and biases. Am I cursing the system that put me up here? Angry that they sent me to the moon in what turned out to be a flawed spacecraft, all because they were hoping for one more feat of desperate glory? Or am I grateful to that system for at least giving me these experiences in the first place? Am I saying a prayer for my eventual safe return? Or do I trust that it will happen through some other means—orbital mechanics or atmospheric drag, or a final trick with the reentry thrusters? Perhaps I'm hoping for one more chance to speak to my wife, my children. You can imagine what you will. Far be it from me to contradict you.

Perhaps I'm thinking of Maresyev, and how I may be sacrificing more than him, at last. A cold comfort, but there is some satisfaction in the thought. Perhaps I'm thinking of Hemingway's old man. The old man went very far out to sea, and when he did, he caught the biggest fish he'd ever seen, but because he'd gone so far, he could not bring it home intact.

I told Blondie that I needed rest, and it is true. I wanted someone to talk to; I wanted to tell my story, and to know what it means. (And I have been telling it! And I trust that you are hearing me, somehow.) But I'm getting tired of storytelling. And I still don't know who you are. And a man needs privacy at certain times, after all.

And it occurs to me: perhaps you already know how it ends! Maybe you have read newspapers or seen television reports telling of my safe rescue by the Chilean Navy; perhaps you have seen a photograph of me climbing a ladder onto one of their ships, flashing my famous grin. And you may have already seen my photograph, the first of its kind, the unimaginable beauty of the earth rising above the moon.

Or perhaps I fell to earth too late. You may have seen footage of the state funeral, or possibly you watched the broadcast live: the somber crowds, the stern men carrying an urn with my ashes to a final resting place in the Kremlin wall, the heavy notes of Mozart's *Requiem* playing all the while. Perhaps they told you the truth. But maybe they had no reason to do so. The spacecraft might have come down on Soviet soil, or tumbled on reentry and disintegrated. Perhaps they simply told you I died in an air crash.

Then again, I might still be up here. That, too, is possible. I don't know when you are reading this. Perhaps all of it is still happening.

Outside I can see the field of stars moving as my spacecraft slowly turns. A tremendous amount of stars, an unimaginable number, stars like you have never seen them— bright and dim and near and far. And far below there is a dark hole, an arc of a circle where the earth is blocking them out. I can tell it is getting smaller, and farther and farther away by the minute.

I start to count the countless stars.

I fall asleep.

I wake up.

I fall asleep.

ACKNOWLEDGMENTS

Many thanks to Francis French for his enthusiasm and support, and his commentary on the finished manuscript.

Dr. Asif Siddiqi's two-volume set *Sputnik and the Soviet Space Challenge* and *The Soviet Space Race with Apollo* remains the definitive English-language history of the Soviet space program, from its curious roots in postwar Germany to the bitter frustration of the failed N-1 program. It's everything history should be: readable, authoritative, well-sourced, and insightful. Not only was his book an invaluable resource, but he also took the time to chat, to read my end product, and to correct a few of my mistakes. I'm very grateful for his feedback and corrections.

Dr. Andrew Jenks' *Yuri Gagarin: The Cosmonaut who Couldn't Stop Smiling* is perhaps the most insightful English-language biography of Yuri Gagarin, as well as an excellent insight into his place in Soviet and Russian culture. Jenks takes a difficult task—digging deep to find the truth of a man who's been shielded in a cocoon of myth—and succeeds admirably. It was the single most valuable source in helping me get a feel for Gagarin as a character; one of the anecdotes in the book even provided me with my title.

Into that Silent Sea and *In the Shadow of the Moon* by Francis French and Colin Burgess did a wonderful job of portraying the relatively unknown personalities who flew Soviet rockets into space—it's a great look at the people behind the posters.

Two Sides of the Moon by Dave Scott and Alexey Leonov was a wonderful dual memoir. In particular, the latter's reminisces about his friend and comrade were touching and moving, a strong reminder of the essential humanity of the man behind the myth. (He also discusses Gagarin's love of *The Old Man and the Sea* in some detail. Though there are some issues with his recounting—he claims to have met Hemingway in Cuba some time after the author's 1961 suicide—this still was an invaluable thematic contribution to my story.) He's also the main source for the anecdote about Korolev's description of his arrest and exile during Stalin's Purges

Boris Chertok's *Rockets and People* was an excellent and candid memoir about the trials and tribulations of the Soviet Union's rocket scientists. His description of their problem-solving methodology was interesting enough that I reproduced it here; his book also pointed me towards several important linguistic discrepancies between American and Russian/Soviet nomenclature. Lastly, it had some great insights into the interplay between Soviet strategic rocketry and space exploration.

James Harford's *Korolev: How One Man Masterminded the Soviet Drive to Beat America to the Moon* is a great biography of the towering and vital man at the center of it all.

Soyuz: A Universal Spacecraft by Rex Hall and David Shayler contained some tremendously valuable information about the Soyuz and Zond spacecraft systems and interiors, as well as some very helpful technical descriptions of in-flight malfunctions on various missions.

Kosmos: A Portrait of the Russian Space Age is a wonderful visual portrayal of the people and places that made the Soviet Union the world's first spacefaring nation. Adam Bartos' photographs are witty and wonderful, and Svetlana Boym's accompanying essay gave valuable insights into the nation's space culture.

Starman: The Truth Behind the Legend of Yuri Gagarin by Jamie Doran and Piers Bizony is an entertaining and informative biography that captures the Gagarin magic while also getting at the contradictions that cropped up in his life in later years. While they perhaps give too much credence to some of the thinly sourced stories about the Soviet space program, it's still a worthwhile read.

The Red Stuff – The True Story of the Russian Race for Space and the accompanying film documentary about Gagarin had some very valuable intervals with the early cosmonauts. It also had some great archival footage of the Soviet space program and the public spectacle which surrounded it.

Yuri Gagarin's own *To the Stars* is somewhat problematic as a historical source. But despite—and perhaps because of—the author's outright lies and omissions, it still provides some valuable insights.

The anonymous contributors to Wikipedia continue to ensure that their site remains a handy and generally reliable reference, but this story highlights some of the intriguing problems with the site, and with history and biography in general. (The Gagarin article claims he was a Christian, but relies on only one source; Jenks insists he wasn't, but acknowledges the pervasiveness of this rumor in recent years. The disputes about such basic facts greatly contributed to my fascination with the Gagarin story, and left me charmed by a man who could remain so long in the public eye while remaining so maddeningly opaque.)

Giano Cromley's been an indispensable companion on the unending voyage that is independent publishing; it'd be a far lonelier journey without him, and I'm tremendously grateful for his feedback and support.

Last, but first. To Octavia, Genesis, and the son whose name has been whittled down to a few intriguing possibilities: you are the most wonderful family a man could ask for, and I love you tremendously.

ABOUT THE AUTHOR

Mr. Brennan earned a B.S. in European History from the United States Military Academy at West Point and an M.S. in Journalism from Columbia University in New York. His writing has appeared in the *Chicago Tribune*, *The Good Men Project*, and *Innerview Magazine*; he's also been a frequent contributor and co-editor at Back to Print and The Deadline. He resides in Chicago.

Follow him on Twitter @jerry_brennan.

ABOUT TORTOISE BOOKS

Slow and steady wins in the end, even in publishing. Tortoise Books is dedicated to finding and promoting quality authors who haven't yet found a niche in the marketplace—writers producing memorable and engaging works that will stand the test of time.

Learn more at www.tortoisebooks.com, or follow us on Twitter @TortoiseBooks.

Printed in the USA
CPSIA information can be obtained
at www.ICGtesting.com
JSHW082352140824
68134JS00020B/2039

9 780998 632513